The Gi

Nine Lives

The Adventures of

Benedict and Blackwell

Book 1

Acknowledgements

I would like to thank Christopher Lynn for his wonderful designs and dedication towards The Adventures of Benedict and Blackwell.

I would also like to thank my parents for constantly giving me their support and love.

Finally, I would like to thank a little ginger cat who gave me his uncompromising love, company and didn't mind sharing his cat biscuits.

Dedicated to Rowan, my light in the dark.

Chapter One

It started with a meow. Then a hiss. And then the unbelievable happened. I watched in horror as his tail twitched and went poker straight.

"Ben!"

"I swear if you're in here, Blackwell, I'm going to rip your pretty little head off!" Sabrina limped in, sweating, pale and furious, another one of her unpractical cream suits ruined by body fluid.

Horror clutched my heart as she saw Ben. An insane and murderous look lit up in her eyes, momentarily paralyzing her.

But it was all he needed. That official letter from the Royal Family, saying that they were visiting our new Campus in Oldbury, wonderfully immortalised in beautiful script and paper of the highest quality was in the perfect spot.

And then it happened. My mouth fell open as Ben did the biggest dump I have ever seen on the PR woman's desk.

A second went by filled with nothing but his purring and the distinct smell of Whiskers.

Without thinking, I grabbed him as Sabrina threw herself across the desk and ran out of the office, her screams bouncing off the walls.

If you're lost by now, I'm talking about my cat.

"It's strange bringing a cat to the office," I know you're saying, but hey- I didn't bring him. Ben does what he likes, whenever he likes, wherever he likes-especially if it disrupts my life.

"I'm going to kill you!" I snarled in his ear, but I knew he was too smug with himself to care about my scolding. "Oh shit, oh shit, oh shit!"

He yawned, breathing cat breath into my face. "I think I improved her office," he meowed.

Ok, ok, I know what you're thinking. Talking cat? I'm going to have to go back to the beginning, aren't I?

My name is Ellie Blackwell. I'm twenty-four and I am officially stuck in my life. By the way- I own a cat that can talk, although he would probably tell you he owned me.

I had moved into a new flat in the town centre, my parents had flown to start their new lives in Australia and my sister was expecting a baby. I was trying my best to make things work, but sometimes things just don't stay where you want them.

I opened my eyes, squinting at the light coming in from the curtains. I groaned and then held my breath, sure I was going to throw up.

"Oh, God," I moaned. I looked at my watch. 7:48am. Unusually, whenever I woke from a hangover, I always did super early for work. I knew I shouldn't have gone out on a Sunday night, but I am very easily swayed.

I unsteadily got to my feet and shuffled to the shower. I would be lying to say I wasn't sick in there between shampooing and conditioning.

Maybe I haven't gone back far enough?

I used to live in Tamworth with my sister and mother. Our dad had gone off a long time ago. I couldn't remember one Christmas or birthday with him- and that wasn't because I had a bad memory- my memory about events, times and places was uncanny. We lived in a semi-detached house, with a cat called Ben. He was a skinny pale ginger cat, who always got into fights. His ears were always crusted with blood and he was constantly snotty. Well, near the end I suppose anyway. I feel guilty even now remembering the state of him. We should have taken him to the vets. But as a child, I always thought that he was just a bit of a fighter- and maybe he was. But looking back now, I think maybe we could have done more.

I loved that cat. He used to follow me to primary school and wait for me to come back, sitting in the garage with me when it rained and my mum had forgotten to hide the back door key for me. He would even share his food with me- yes, I ate cat biscuits, and they were delicious.

We took him to the move with us to Nuneaton, and I think that was where his health started to go downhill. He was very old by that point- eighteen years my mum had told me. I remembered when we gave him his first bath in the new house. He was starting to get pretty filthy and couldn't clean himself. He was so scared he wet himself. We went on holiday, and mum gave him to a woman with four other cats to look after. When we came back, mum said he was happy there and we should leave him.

I didn't want to leave him, but he didn't have much of a life in our house. He was only allowed to stay in the kitchen. I think he was always a reminder to mum of our biological dad. Barry had brought him home one day as a kitten. Mum hated anything Barry brought home, but even she had to admit it was different from the cars and motorbikes he kept dragging back.

I saw Ben as much as I could after school and throughout the holidays. He was getting skinnier and skinnier. One day I came over to the woman's house- I can't remember her name now, and she said that Ben hadn't been home all day

"He was sitting on the windowsill yesterday looking out for you," she said, her charms and bracelets rattling as she made me some orange juice.

Going back, maybe it was cruel of her to say that he was looking for me, because I always felt guilty afterwards. I felt as though I had let him down. That one day I hadn't come to see him, was the day he ran away.

I searched for him in tears with my older cousin, Craig, who found it hilarious. We went into people's back gardens, searching for him. We came across a pond and Craig said, "Maybe he fell in there and drowned."

I was furious and inconsolable. I returned to my auntie's house where my family was, burying myself into a hug from my mum.

"Sometimes, Ellena, cats go away when it's time for them to pass on," she said.

More tears followed, more searches, until days passed on and he didn't return. I wondered whether my mum had taken him to the vet to be put down, but she always denied it. I had to accept the fact that Ben was gone. I would dream about him sometimes. I would promise him I would give him a better life. Treat him like a king. I was older now, wiser too (though my family may have said otherwise) and I realised that maybe we hadn't given him the life he had deserved.

Thirteen years passed. I left school, went to college, went to university, back to college, and finally came back to Warwickshire. Life moved so quickly, and I already felt I had lived a number of different lives.

My love life was non-existent, my friends were not exactly plentiful and my job was stuck.

I worked as a Teaching Assistant at the U.C.W (University College of Warwickshire) where I had built my own hopes and dreams, only to return there to assure other dreamers they could make it in a world of concrete and One Direction.

I was returning home from work, thoroughly depressed after having my hours slashed in half. The Student Support Team always reassured us that there were more hours to be had, and then would hire more staff, to then cut down on hours saying that there wasn't enough. I had been there nearly a year, and still hadn't nabbed the contract I desperately craved. I needed stability; I was turning twenty-five that year for God's sake! I wanted to get on the property ladder, get a better car than my crappy KA that my uncle was insisting he was still getting around to fixing, and I desperately wanted someone to share it all with.

Little did I know I was going to get that someone sooner than I thought.

I fumbled in my bag for my keys, my hands freezing from my fingerless gloves. It took an age as usual because my bag is full of crap. I pulled them out, wondering about how I was going to pay my rent next month. My flat was like any other flat. Average. I had only been in there a few months, previously living with my parents. But when they said they were moving to Australia, I saw it as good sense to get out of the house so they could prepare to sell. More fool I, because my sister moved straight in with her husband and huge bump.

The flat was second floor on a set of terrace houses that aside from a patch of gated grass at the front, was straight on the main road. It cost a fortune in gas, mainly because I refuse to be cold at any time, and a fortune in maltesers- mainly because that's what I eat when I'm depressed.

I shivered and struggled to find the right key out of my collection. That's when I saw him.

A pale ginger cat was sitting at my front door, wet and miserable looking in the drizzle that fell. His eyes stared at me, pale orange, blood at his ears from fighting, two small bald patches on his temples.

My lungs didn't even pull in a breath at that moment.

He was a spitting image of Ben.

I stared back at him and without thinking knelt down. "Hello," I said in my best cat voice (we all have one). The cat came immediately, running his wet back under my hands. Grit came away with some fur and I wrinkled my nose in distaste He was filthy. I stood up, the Ben-look-a-like rubbing himself on my legs. I put the key into the door and as soon as I opened it, he shot in.

I swore under my breath, but I knew I would have let him in sooner or later. It was miserable outside and I was a sucker for cats. I walked in, dropping my bag by the door and taking off my wet coat. The cat was sniffing his way around my flat, rubbing against my furniture and shaking himself free from the rain.

Throwing off my gloves, I rushed into the kitchen to turn on the heating before I dealt with the cat. I turned around to find him sitting on the floor in front of me, staring at me expectantly.

He meowed.

God he looked like Ben.

"You hungry?" I said.

He meowed again.

I bit my lip, thinking. I pulled out a small dish and started rooting through my cupboards. I found a tin of tuna and quickly emptied its contents. I didn't even like tuna, so I had no idea why it was in my cupboard. I set it on the floor for him to leap to his banquet. Watching him wolf it down, I set down another saucer of watered down milk.

I watched him eat, memories of Tamworth surfaced at the sight of this cat. It was obvious it couldn't be Ben. I was eleven when he went walkabouts and that was nearly fourteen years ago. The cat would have to be thirty-two years old for it to Ben. I knelt down next to him and scratched behind his ear.

"But you do look like Ben," I cooed to him.

He stopped eating and shoved his head into my hand, purring. It was nice until he wiped his snotty nose on me.

"Eugh."

I cleaned up the blood from him as best as I could with paper towels and wiped his wet nose. I even gave him a brush through and wiped his coat free from oil and grit. Soon he was looking presentable.

I sat down on the sofa for him to jump into my lap. He was still a bit smelly, but I carried on stroking him. I did play with the thought of calling the RSPCA but I couldn't bring myself to reach for the phone.

I put on the TV, and wrapped a blanket around us both. Soon Ben was stretched out, purring and licking my hand. I realised with a jerk that I had named him Ben without even knowing it.

"Would you like that?" I said to him, tickling his chin. "Would you like to be called Ben?"

His purring sounded snotty, so I cuddled him even more.

And it was decided. He had chosen me. And if you think he chose me as an owner, you would be very much mistaken. I was the owned human.

Weeks passed of attempting to get more hours at work to no avail. Yeah, they had given me an extra two hour slot, but what did that pay for? Not much considering the cost of the vets. Ben's cold went and his coat started looking better, not to mention he had started putting on weight. Over the stress at work, I had lost nearly half a stone, preferring to grab a quick soup and then go back to work to teach at night. I only teach twice a week in the evenings, but I knew I would do more if they asked me. I was desperately trying to build myself up as an English teacher but had to admit even though I loved it, I needed something more stable.

My work was always reluctant to give contracts out to employees. I think it was so they could have more control over the support staff. They knew we were desperate for more hours and would jump through hoops for them. They always promised us hours over the summer, and then would give them to contracted staff. I felt as though it was time they gave me a contract- after a year of working there, surely? I didn't know how to broach it.

I started drinking at night, feeling sorry for myself. Trying to keep myself together over Skype calls with my parents in Australia. They wanted me to come over, but I had screwed that up as well. I had a visa stamped to go over, but I had turned it down after spending a few months over there. I had been homesick. And when we had returned from Australia, my Granddad had been really ill. We discovered he had cancer, and after weeks of caring for him, he passed away. It had nearly destroyed me. But it was January now, start of a new year and time to move on, or so my dad kept telling me. But it was the anniversary of his death in February, and each day it came nearer, I struggled.

Confused that I mentioned the word, "dad"? Well, that's my stepdad, Andy. He came along when I was ten after the divorce of my parents. He was the best thing that happened to my family. He made my mother happy, and in 2003 after years of dating, they finally got married. I called him Andy face to face, because that name will always mean more to me than 'dad'. To say the word 'dad' and expect a response made my stomach turn, memories of slamming doors and a motorcycle going off in the distance rife in my mind. *Andy* was a word that made me feel safe. Even to call out the word, "dad" felt alien and unnatural. It made me feel self-conscious.

I called my biological father Barry. It made things easier. He had lived a double life with us, having another family. We didn't find out until we moved to Nuneaton that he had children with another woman. To my knowledge, they still didn't know we existed, and that was tough to take. Sometimes in my life, the subject of Barry would crop up and I would torture myself over it. I would try and search for the children on the internet. I had upset my mother recently by asking how she would feel if I one day met up with them. She was appalled; believing anything that came from Barry would be a bad seed, my sister and I not included.

Sometime Kayleigh and I would just tell people that we were an immaculate birth. It made Mum laugh, and I think she preferred the idea.

Ben coming along had brought Tamworth back, but funnily enough, he reminded me of the good parts of my childhood. Reminded me that it wasn't all bad. And it wasn't. We had a great childhood- mum made sure of that. I had a Barbie every birthday and every Christmas, and once a year- maybe even twice, she would take us to McDonalds. We were always dressed nicely- yeah, so they were clothes from charity shops and carboots and hand-me-downs, but she always made sure we looked presentable. I wondered how she managed sometimes. How she kept things together. But then I remembered seeing the cracks in her plight, and then would try to think of something else. It was a dark hole I didn't want to fall into.

But it seemed I was already in a black hole- the black hole of being terribly hung-over. I looked in the mirror after the shower and agreed that I looked awful. Ben seemed to agree, staring at me disapprovingly as I got dressed and dried my hair.

I was going to make things work for me at the U.C.W. I needed to network my way into making a success. Things seemed to go well when I made things happen- see who I could talk to, do favours for, search for work in different departments.

But I had been shaken recently. I had been asked to take up I.T classes at the college with an hour before teaching my English Class. I finished late at night and was expected to prepare to teach I.T to a group of 2nd Year Business students the next day.

My restlessness had made me go in, too scared to say no, wanting to make an impression, and feeling as though if I didn't take on the workload, then they wouldn't give me any more work in the future. I would be a failure. Incompetent.

I had stayed up late at night and had gotten up early to prepare for the lesson I had no idea how to teach. But I'm good at blagging. I had gone in, seemingly confident and assured, exhausted from searching for the information I needed, no help given from the staff and delivered the lesson. The lesson had gone well and the students seemed to like me. Three weeks passed of me delivering this course, desperately trying to find out more about Excel. I knew Publisher, Powerpoint, Word and even Photoshop, but Access and Excel were things I found difficult to grasp.

"Excuse me," I said, knocking on an office door a busy colleague had pointed out. A few women looked up from their work, their desks heaped with work and empty cups of tea. "I was wondering who I could talk to about Excel?"

"You want Maggie," a woman from Childcare said, dark rings under her eyes from lack of sleep. "But she's not here." The smile didn't reach her eyes and I knew she didn't have any time for me. She had her own problems to deal with the day. My heart sank. I needed help with this, but somehow I knew it wasn't going to come from these women.

A manic and nervous energy hummed in the room- too much caffeine and too many papers. The walls were covered in timetables, equality and diversity posters and to do lists. The calendar of hunks was a window of optimistic hope in the corner. I found my eyes lingering on it.

I went to the manager, Jeff, who had hinted at further opportunities for answers. In all honesty, I was a positive thinker- and it was the hope of achieving something more that made me stay at the U.C.W. But I knew my needs were unimportant to the place. I was as easily replaceable as a coaster on a coffee table. He had made me hopeful, as a few months back I had had an interview with him about teaching English Functional Skills. I was still waiting to start this, but I didn't want to push too much in case I pissed him off.

"Maggie's great," he said, his grey suit immaculate. He was new at the college, probably around mid-fifties and I could tell the strain was getting to him. The college was very disorganised, and I could tell he had a lot to deal with. A part of me felt sorry for him, wishing that I already knew the answer so I wouldn't have to bother anyone. I hated feeling like a burden. It made me feel incapable.

I nodded, not getting the information I needed. I returned after that several times, asking for help about the course, asking for information.

"I was wondering how do I know how to mark their work?" I asked the woman who had heaped the load on me, Sandra. She was busy, I could tell and didn't have much energy to help a flustered trainee teacher.

"You can find it online," she said dismissively.

"Ok..." I said slowly. "I was wondering as well, that job Jeff gave me for English Functional Skills, do you know when I'll start doing it?"

She looked confused, and I had no idea why- she had been there in the interview with Jeff. "This is it," she said, pointing to the I.T folder clutched in my arms.

"What?"

"The job you're doing now- that's the job you applied for."

"I applied for English Functional Skills," I said, my grip hardening on those hated papers, my fake smile slipping.

"Oh, that's gone now. There aren't any jobs."

My heart sank harder and I felt panic start to rise. I returned to the Student Support Office to sign out, her words repeating in my head. I felt duped. Stupid. A fool.

"How are you, Ellie?" the manager Janet asked absently as I returned some student forms to a file cabinet.

"Fine, thank you," I replied, because it was expected. I plastered a fake smile to my face, matching her own. "I was wondering if there were any hours available for me at all?"

Janet wanted to talk to me somewhere private then.

"To be honest," she said, motioning for me to sit down, "we're reluctant to give you any more hours in case you start doing more teaching."

I tried not to frown. "Right..."

"So I'm sorry but there's not much I can do."

That faint bubbling of panic started to rise up in my chest again. "But I don't think I'll be doing anymore teaching," I said, "It's a lot at the moment-"

"Sorry," Janet interrupted. "There's nothing I can do."

I returned home, miserable and set on marking English work. When I had finished that, I fed Ben, cleaned the house and then started preparing for the next I.T lesson, researching Excel and Access, trying to come up with interesting lesson plans that would appeal to business students.

A week later, I snapped. I was crying every day and had started to think darkly. How easy it would be to simply veer off the road when I was driving? How easy it would be to fall down the stairs. I could escape that way.

The thoughts scared me. I was more upset at the thought that I could even think of doing that to my family, imagining their faces, their reactions. How selfish I would be to even think of it.

It was a cold that made me call in sick for work. My body was wracked with guilt that I was letting my students down, but a relief seeped into my bloodstream that I had a full 24 hours to be away from the place that made me feel so badly.

I went to the doctors simply to get more of my pill. Seeing my aunt's car in the car park (she worked as the manager there) I popped into the office whilst I waited for the nurse.

She looked concerned as soon as I walked in. I can remember everything about that heavy feeling inside my gut- a sensation that I was floating almost and that the only way I could physically get out of work if something terrible happened to me- then it wouldn't be my fault. I wouldn't be weak. It would be an accident, unavoidable- they couldn't make me go back then and I wouldn't be able to make myself go back.

"You've lost weight," she said, her head cocked to the side with a smile that said 'I'm concerned about you'.

I eased into conversation about work, and then it happened. I broke down. I started crying and told her everything, feeling so god damn weak, weak, *weak*.

There was a hot feeling in my face that said even though I had drenched my shirt in tears, there was still a tidal wave to come. My chest heaved in a silent and uncontrollable wracking sob that wouldn't seem to stop.

The next thing I knew, I was sitting in front of a doctor, feeling foolish and uncomfortable.

"I'm sorry," was the first thing I said to him.

In his face was a kindness that saved me.

When he told me I was suffering with anxiety and depression, a strange sensation washed over me. This was something I had heard other people suffer from- not me. Surely this was just real life? Wasn't this how everyone felt?

He wanted to sign me off for six weeks. It seemed obscene. He was adamant and so was I. I had students, deadlines, managers to prove something to and other co-workers to compete with. I couldn't stay away that long.

I held that sick note in my hand, seeing the six weeks wrote there in black ink and then crossed out reluctantly, an amendment of '3 weeks' below instead.

My aunt held my hand afterwards.

"You can't go back," she said. "Stack shelves, Ellena, be a waitress-anything. Don't do this. It'll kill you."

But I had focused my entire education towards this job. How could I no longer want it? I was scared to call my work. But I was even more terrified to go back.

I got back to my flat and stood at the window, the radiator burning my legs. I dialled the number before I could think about it, the sick note clutched in my sweating hand.

Thoughts plagued my mind. I would be giving up all of that hard work... I would come across as someone who was weak...

Incompetent.

Incompetent.

Incompetent.

It was a relief to finally have people on my side. For all what the University College of Warwickshire was like, the HR Department were brilliant. They sorted everything out whilst I was crying on the phone, apologising, explaining, and apologising some more.

I didn't go into work for three weeks.

It was too much. My hours being slashed. The job I applied for not existing. Being given a position, not because it was something I applied for, but because another teacher didn't want to do it. I felt lied to, taken for granted- a scapegoat for the contracted tutors and other staff to dump their workload on- get rid of the problems that they didn't want to deal with. Not being supported. But I was the one feeling guilty. Was this what teaching was all about? Was it truly like this? I had dreamed of being a teacher for years, and I felt now I had gotten what I wanted, I couldn't handle it. I couldn't handle the real world. Why wasn't I coping?

I felt ashamed to say I was off work from depression and anxiety. I wanted to lock myself in my house and tell no one. Just vanish for a while. I was worried about telling my family, telling my sister. I was scared she wouldn't want me around the baby when he was born. Worried that my dad would think I was being silly.

Most of all, I was worried about the sick note running out.

The doctor gave me pills, but I didn't want to take them. They stayed in my cupboard collecting dust as I sat at home, Ben curled up on my lap as I applied for other jobs.

Whatever thoughts I had about my family, I was wrong. They were so supportive of me. But when I went over to my sister's to see my mother, freshly returned from Australia to be there for the birth of the baby, I could see the worry in her eyes.

Three weeks passed and I spent the time refilling my batteries by doing the things I enjoyed. I read, I ate, I saw family and I did a couple of open mic nights. Crowds were a difficulty. Panic would rise in my chest as soon as too many people surrounded me. People's faces who I knew were no longer friendly. Glances were taken as dirty looks. Environments I used to feel safe in became dark abysses I wanted to escape from.

But I improved. I became happy again and determined to prove everything wrong- I was cured. I was fine.

Just *fine*.

The three weeks went and my doctor wanted me to take more time off.

"I'm ok," I said, an urgency in me rising to get back to work- get back to my career. I could make it work. I could.

"You must be careful," he said slowly, "not to go back before you are ready. Many people go back too soon."

Of course I knew more than this highly educated man that had potentially saved my life.

I argued with him and we finally compromised me to go back on a phased return. He agreed to write my health note, making me promise him to return if it didn't work out.

I had a meeting with Jeff. He promised me support. He promised me a learning mentor to help me with the course. He promised me some hours teaching English at the other campus. I was happy, agreeing, apologising and feeling hopeful.

I returned to work, ready to get help on Excel.

"Hiya," I said coming into the Foundation Learning Office. My anxiety pricked up immediately.

"Hi Ellie," said Sandra spotting me. But she seemed to say my name for too long. Her eyes knowing what had happened. I felt like she was talking to me like I was an unstable student. Someone weak. Or maybe I was just paranoid. "You ok?"

Again, her words were drawn out too long. *Youuuu ooookkkkkaaayyy?*

"Yes thank you," I said, unable to hold eye contact any longer. I was relieved when she left. "Erm," I said to the remaining women, noticing one who had been pointed out as Maggie, "I was wondering if someone could help me with Excel."

Maggie's green eyes peered at me from a tanned face. Dark curls were cut into a sharp bob with a thick Asian print scarf wrapped around her shoulders. Paranoia slammed into my brain. She didn't like me. She didn't think anything of me. She thought I was just a young woman coming in to an office that she had ruled in for so long, daring to ask for help. She wanted to make an example of me. Wanted to make me feel inadequate.

She knew.

She knew.

She knew.

My chest heaved, my brain working in overdrive. Suddenly everyone knew everything about me. Knew how weak I was. How I was crumbling. They knew I couldn't survive. I was a nobody.

They knew.

They knew.

They knew.

"What do you mean?" she asked.

"I need some excel papers for my students in IT Functional Skills," I said unsteadily. I knew Jeff had spoken to her. Told her the situation. I knew she knew who I was.

"What sort of papers?" she asked again, her own stack in front of her. Lesson plans, marking and schedules were scattered in front of her, pens overflowing and claustrophobic in their pot. A half-eaten sandwich was in front of her, a cup of tea gone cold, a skin already floating on top.

"I need..." I swallowed, my mouth and throat unbelievably dry. I tried again. "Just some papers to introduce excel to them," I said.

"They're over there," she said, gesturing to an entire wall of filing cabinets with a book still in her hand.

I stood there awkwardly, staring at the wall of metal drawers. I couldn't bring myself to step forward.

Please help me.

"Which drawer?" I asked, trying to keep my voice steady.

"Top one."

I let out a tense breath and opened the first drawer I came to. Thousands of papers sat there, suffocating with plastic wallets and paper folders.

I didn't know where to start. For a moment, all I could see was paper. My hands started running through them, my brain panicking.

I don't know what I'm looking for, I don't know what I'm looking for!

"Can you help me?" I asked her, the words costing me more breath I needed to keep my heart pumping.

"Well what do you need?" she asked, looking as though she would rather be doing anything else than talking to a useless girl.

Useless.

Useless.

Useless.

"I don't know." I put a hand over my face then, feeling heat rise to my cheeks. "I have never taught excel, the students have never done it, I just need someone to help me pick some papers."

"Well they're all in there."

I can't do this.

"Ok, I'll be back in a moment." I knew then, I had seconds to get out of that hated office before I started to cry.

She said something else, but I was out of the door.

I'll do it on my own, I thought. *I'll just do it on my own. It'll be easier.*

When I got home, I fed Ben and cried. He watched me as I bawled my eyes out and licked the salt from my hands occasionally, stinking of tuna.

I called HR and told them I wasn't going to teach IT anymore. That I was promised support and I wasn't getting it. That the students deserved a tutor who knew what they were doing and that I was sorry. Sorry. Sorry. Sorry.

I started to have panic attacks and stayed away from the few friends I had. Soon, it was as if I was forgotten. I didn't want to socialise, I didn't want to eat, and I didn't want to leave the house.

That was when it happened.

My best friends were Ben and Captain Morgan. I was sitting on the sofa, crying at Beauty and the Beast, wrapped in a blanket with empty packets of chocolate around me.

"Oh for the love of *God*!" exclaimed a voice. "Will you desist from making that horrible noise?!"

The voice was coming from my lap.

I looked down, a malteser falling from my mouth.

"Yes, that's right, I said it- and I'll say it again!" Ben hissed. "Stop stuffing your face with chocolate, stop crying and will you switch off this God awful film?!"

"*Ben*?!"

He sniffed. "Actually, my name is Benedict."

"Wha-?"

I stood, unceremoniously tipping him from my lap. I looked at the glass of rum and coke in my hand and then back at him.

"Benedict?" I slurred, "But I called you Ben!"

"Your pig of a father called me Ben," he sniffed, idly licking a paw. "But my name is Benedict."

"Benedict?"

"Yes?"

"You're Ben?"

"Yes."

I stared at him, my eyes trembling in my skull as I clutched the glass of rum harder. "You're *Ben*?"

"No- Benedict, but I am also Ben."

"Ben Ben, as if in *Ben*?" That moment was the first moment in my life that I was to witness a cat rolling his eyes. Then it clicked. "You can t*alk*?!"

"Well-"

I screamed then and ran into my room. I stared at the door, unable to comprehend that a cat was shouting my name and calling me a "stupid human."

"*Lalalalalalalalalalala lalala la la la*!" I shouted with my back against the door and my hands over my ears.

"Just so you know," he said, "that is the worst song I have ever heard."

"What do you know about songs?!" I yelled. "You're a *cat*!"

The scratching stopped. "I love music. I know a couple of songs- would you like to hear?"

"Go away!" I shouted. "*Lalalalala la la lalala*!"

"*Meoooooowwww! Meowowow, meow meowwwwwwww! memeowmeow meoooooooowwww*!"

"Lalala la la LA LA LA LA!"

"MEOOOOOOWWWW! MEOOW MEOWW MEMEMEOWWWWWWW!"

"Stop it!" I sobbed. "Stop it!"

"Only if you stop it and let me in!"

"No!"

"MEOOOOOOWWWW! MEOOOOOOWWWW! MEOW MEOWW MEMEMEOWWWWWWW! MEOWW MEOWW MEMEMEOWWWWWWW!"

The meowing continued and the neighbours starting banging on the wall. I pulled my hands from my ears. "All right! All right!"

"Meow?"

"You win!" I yelled wrenching the door open.

The ginger cat sat before me, looking incredibly smug. "I win?"

"Yes!" I snarled.

"Then I best explain, hadn't I?"

Chapter Two

Sitting down at the table was the strangest thing with a cat. He paced back and forth until he was comfortable and swished his tail around him.

"This can't go on, Ellena," he said.

I blinked. "What?"

"This self-pitying cycle."

"I'm not self pitying!"

"You're crying over a Disney film."

I folded my arms across my chest, affronted. "Everyone knows Disney films are brutal."

You're talking to a cat. You're talking to a cat. You're talking to a cat!

I got to my feet and picked up the bottle of rum. Maybe I was hallucinating? How drunk really was I?

"Yes, you're very drunk," Ben said, sounding bored.

"You're a cat."

"Yes."

"A talking cat?"

He looked amused and watched me as I poured another glass. "I would say that isn't a good idea but you would do it anyway."

"I'm talking to a cat."

"So?"

I faltered. "It's not natural!"

"Who says so?"

"The world!"

"Maybe we can all talk," Ben said. "Maybe I was just so sick of your behaviour that I decided I would talk to you."

"But you're *Ben*!"

"Benedict."

"You know what I mean- you're Ben from Tamworth!"

"And you're Ellena from Tamworth."

"But- but you ran away!"

He tilted his head. "Did I?"

"Did you what?" God I was so confused. My head was spinning, my hands were shaking and my slippered feet were sweating.

"Run away?"

"Yes!"

"What makes you think I ran away?" he meowed whilst stretching. "Maybe it was just time for me to go."

I frowned. It was impossible for him to still be alive- and more impossible that he could talk. "But you're back?"

"Yes."

"Why? How?"

"You need me," he said simply. "You're my human."

The next day, I woke, finding myself wrapped in cat and blankets. If I was expecting to be talking cat free, I was very much mistaken. Ben seemingly had decided that he had been quiet too long and enjoyed too much being the soul of conversation.

"Make sure you have some breakfast," he said as I poured a cup of tea for myself. "It's lovely outside- not that I want to go outside. Horrible muck that humans drop littering the streets. Maybe I will take a walk though? A wee stroll in the park mayhaps? See some birds? Maybe I can walk you to work? That would be nice, wouldn't it? Like old times? I remember-"

And it went on. His cat voice meowing and crooning as I prepared myself for work, as I ate, as I showered and as I dressed. I nodded and ummed my way through his conversation, shock still paralysing my limbs from doing what I needed them. I dropped my brush about five times whilst trying to brush my hair.

"You're blonde now. I like it. I think you should go ginger though, like me. We could match then."

Whether the nightmare of him talking to me would stop, I didn't know. I wondered if someone had spiked my drink at work, or maybe I had drank a bad batch of rum- or maybe some cells had just exploded in my brain, making me think that my cat could talk to me.

"Aren't you going to say bye?" Ben asked as I unlocked the door to go out.

I froze in my steps and saw his swish his tail in anticipation. "Bye," I said, and shut the door.

The cold air brought some life into my arms and legs as I power walked it to work, determined to stamp out any anxiety in my body. My car still hadn't been fixed and with the frost of the floor, the short walk to work had taken ten minutes longer to avoid falling over.

Suddenly, I tripped. I looked down and saw Ben rub himself along my legs.

"I thought I would walk you to work," he said cheerfully.

My eyes widened and I looked wildly about. "How did you get out?" I hissed.

"You left the bathroom window open after your shower," he said, sniffing the air. "Come on, you're going to be late else." He started walking ahead of me and then turned around. "Come on!"

I walked up to him. "Go home!"

"Don't be silly," he said. "It's boring back there."

My eyes scanned my surroundings and saw a group of school kids walking towards us in a group, laughing and talking loudly.

"But you said it was mucky out here!"

His tail went up in interest at the school kids. "They're loud," he noted.

"Go home!" I rubbed my forehead and stopped. "Oh god, I'm talking to a cat."

Ben walked close to my leg as the group of teenagers approached. "Nice cat!" one of the kids shouted at me.

My mouth worked but nothing would come out. The teenagers stopped walking and barred my way from walking past them. It was a narrow path and the road was busy. For a moment, worry flamed up for Ben as I watched them pet him.

He enjoyed the attention, and I rolled my eyes.

"Is he yours?" a young girl asked wearing a skirt that I deemed a bit too short for school in this weather.

"Um... yeah," I said.

"What's he doing out?" another teenager asked.

"Walking me to work?" I offered weakly. They loved it, petted Ben some more and watched me walk away with him.

"Well that was nice," Ben remarked, tail high in the air.

I said nothing, still trying to stop myself from having a total meltdown.

I allowed him to walk with me to work, figuring that if I did then he would be happy and just go home.

"Ok Ben," I said at the gates to the college, uncomfortable with the amount of U.C.W students staring at me. "Time to go now."

"Don't be silly, I'll walk you to the door," he said, taking off again.

I had no choice but to follow, noticing every look, whisper and pointed finger in my direction. I nervously smiled at the students, nodded and said good morning.

"Nice pussy," one student said, his chav mates laughing around him. Ben hissed at them, much to their amusement and my satisfaction.

"Mind your language," I said, revealing my staff badge.

There wasn't a more smug cat as I walked to the doors of reception. I looked down at Ben then and worried about him getting back. I frowned and bent down to him. "Ok then Ben, time to go home."

His tail twitched as he blinked at me. He didn't say anything, and I suppose it was because a group of students just walked past me, murmuring the word, "cat".

"Home time, Ben," I said, making my voice sound pleasant in front of the students. "Go on. *Go home!*"

He purred at me and thrust his head into my hand.

I stroked him quickly and then stood up. "Bye bye, Ben."

"Have a good day at work!" he meowed as I turned around to walk into the building. I jumped, but as I looked back he was gone, and the students were absent also.

I frowned. Trust him to choose his moments.

Chapter Three

Hoping to repair any burst brain cells that had made me able to hear Ben talk, I threw myself into work. I was going to make things happen for myself. In my break, I created a six week Creative Writing Course. If the U.C.W weren't going to make things happen for me, I was going to make things happen for myself.

I emailed it to a couple of schools in the area, saying that I have developed a course suitable for students doing or preparing for their G.C.S.E's in English who needed some extra help in their creative writing. I also wanted to inspire young writers- that was always my passion. Being a Teaching Assistant just paid the bills. It was writing I truly loved.

After I had done that, (I had a two hour break) I emailed all of the schools in the area, emailing them my C.V and asked about any upcoming vacancies. I finished with applying for a couple of jobs and went back to class actually feeling good about myself.

At half four I had finished work. I needed to prepare for my English lesson. I walked into the staff room and signed out, when a line of conversation caught my ear.

"...ginger cat outside."

"What was that?" I asked.

A teaching assistant (whose name I don't know) smiled at me. "Oh, we were just saying that there's a ginger cat outside reception."

My heart stopped. "Oh god."

The TA looked confused. "Don't you like cats?"

"Not that one."

I walked outside to find Ben sitting there, licking his paws clean from whatever he had dared to step on.

He blinked as my shoulder got in the way of his sun and started to rub himself on my legs. "Good day at work?"

"Didn't you go back to the flat?" I said through clenched teeth, aware that people were looking at me from the reception windows.

He didn't answer me and decided to meow instead as a couple of students walked past. "Shall we go home?" he finally said as they were out of earshot.

I looked behind and saw a couple of TA's standing there murmuring to each other whilst gawping at me. They waved then, grinning and I was forced to wave back.

"Let's go," I said, quickly jet setting off into my fastest powerwalk.

He walked me to work for the rest of the week and was there waiting for me when I finished. People had started to talk about it around the college, but Student Support never said a word.

The next week, I found a bowl of milk for him by the reception doors, and soon someone was feeding him as well. Concerned that they thought he was a stray, I decided to broach the subject of a collar.

"Don't be ridiculous," he sniffed. "Me? Wear a collar? Never in my life!"

I had grown used to the fact that whatever brain cells that had been damaged weren't going to repair themselves, and resigned to the fact that I lived with a talking cat.

"What about a really nice collar?"

"Oh sorry, were you considering putting me in a horrid one?"

"Ben!"

He jumped away from me and onto the windowsill, his pale ginger back as my only response. I rolled my eyes. "*Benedict*?"

His tail twitched. "That's better," he said, quickly returning.

"But what if someone catches you?"

"That is impossible."

He was right, you know.

A week or so later, we were to test this theory. Whether Ben had become bored waiting outside for me in the cold, or whether he decided he would like to invade my life even more, he decided to take his intrusion one step further.

I was in the library, replying to Nuneaton Academy. They had expressed an interest in my Creative Writing Program and wanted to meet me for a discussion. My hours were still low at the college, but things had become so much better since I had stopped teaching I.C.T. Jeff however, didn't seem to want to reply to my emails about any upcoming work. Whether he had given me up as a lost cause, or too much trouble to deal with, I don't know. All I knew that it was nigh on impossible to get his attention.

"Oh my God, is that a *cat*?"

I looked up tiredly, wondering which student had just discovered the old news that a cat liked to sit outside the reception (the library was above reception), from looking out of the window. I realised then that the red haired student in question was actually looking down the English Literature Section.

My eyes widened.

"No.you.*haven't*!" I stood from my seat and heard another student shriek with delight. "Oh god, oh god, oh god!"

I turned around and saw the Library Assistants soon clock on. "Did someone say there's a cat in here?" one with a 90's red bob and diamante glasses demanded. Her co-worker with curly hair stared back at her in confusion.

I picked up my bag and quickly logged off. I was getting out of here!

Then I heard it. That meow. I turned around to see a Library Assistant lunge for a ball of ginger fur, only to fall into a trolley full of returned books. My eyes widened, half shocked that someone was throwing themselves around, and half because that ball of fur was darting around students' feet, whom of which were still shrieking and yelling with delight. The sanctity of quiet was soon destroyed in the library as I watched nigh near the entire staff try and catch the cat.

My cat.

"Get him!" 90's bob woman shouted.

Now, if there's a time to regret not getting out of there while you can, then this was the time, because that ball of fur, suddenly clocked me.

I just managed to drop my bag as it flew in my direction and threw itself into my arms, purring all too loudly.

Without saying a word, I turned and walked out- and into Jeff.

Jeff was wearing another one of his impeccable grey suits, which I realised to dismay had quickly become covered in Ben's ginger fur.

"Oh, hi, Jeff," I said, clutching Ben tightly to me, terrified he'd run off again and cause more madness.

Jeff's face was unreadable, and soon I was surrounded by Librarians.

"Is this your cat?" 90's bob demanded.

"No animals allowed!"

"Look at the state of the library!"

My mouth worked as Ben purred into my ear, his eyes half closed in satisfaction. "Um, I'm, err-"

"Is this the cat I've been hearing so much about?" Jeff demanded, his arms becoming crossed over his chest.

I glanced at the Librarians, smug expressions on their faces, smelling discipline about to be dealt.

"Um, possibly?" I said, my heart pounding, aware that my lunch had fallen out of my bag.

A moment's pause came before the shocking happened.

Jeff smiled. "How's he finding the whiskers?"

"Wha-?"

"The whiskers?" Jeff prompted again. "I leave whiskers outside for him. Don't worry- the milk isn't proper milk- it's cat's milk for kittens. My wife bought it when she heard about your cat. She says they love it."

I think the expression I had on my face was reflected on the surrounding Librarians around.

"And you lot," he growled, turning to the library staff. "Whatever pandemonium you started in the

Library was appalling, disruptive and unnecessary. It's a cat- not a rhino!"

90's bob started to splutter. "But, he was disrupting the students, sir!"

Jeff snorted, making me jump. "Nonsense. You disrupted the students. Don't let it happen again. Ellie? May I have a word?"

Numb, I nodded and started to follow him into his office as the army of Librarian's dispersed.

"Um, Ellie?"

"Yes?"

"Is that your ham sandwich on the floor?"

Quickly retrieving my lunch, I followed Jeff into his office and sat, Ben curling up into a nice warm ball on my lap.

"Right now, Ellie, I understand things haven't been easy recently," he said, "but you really can't bring a cat to work with you."

"Would you believe me if I said he brought himself?" I had no way to properly explain myself and I didn't expect to get away with this. I was screwed.

Jeff laughed to my surprise, making me jump. "Actually, I could probably believe that."

"He walks me to work," I blurted, realising how crazy it sounded as soon as I said it. "And he waits for me to finish here. I think he gets bored."

Jeff frowned. "Don't you keep him in the house?"

If only it was that simple. "He's an escape artist. If you kept him in this office, he'd find a way out."

For some reason, Jeff found that hilarious as well. I was so confused and embarrassed, until Jeff started to show me some pictures on his phone of his own cats.

"Five?" I said, trying not to gasp it out. "You have five cats?"

"We did have six, but Tilly got ran over."

An awkward silence passed at Jeff stared into space. I sensed that even Ben was starting to get a bit uncomfortable.

"Anyway," Jeff started, making me jump again, "I have seen your emails, and I've been meaning to get back to you. I believe you've started doing a Creative Writing Course outside of the U.C.W?"

I shifted in my seat in discomfort. "Yes," I said slowly. "I work part time and I like to stay pro-active." I smiled, realising that I had said something very grown up and then tried to look serious- difficult with a ginger cat in your lap. "I've been meaning to ask you actually, Jeff, since we're here now face to face..."

"Yes...?"

I then launched into my idea of running a Creative Writing competition within the college. I said that I knew that there weren't any courses to actually cater to this, and that we only had GCSE English or Foundation English, but that may play to our favour.

That we may be tapping into unknown talent. The college prided itself on its Art Campus in the neighbouring town and catered to everything except from Creative Writing.

"It could be something that may be pursued in the future," I said. "I've noticed AQA have started to deliver an A-Level Creative Writing Course. This could be just the thing to bring up interest."

Jeff frowned, and I wondered if I had gone too far with him. Been too ambitious.

"The college doesn't deliver A-Levels, Ellie," he said thoughtfully. "But it's a good idea. I see no reason why we can't hold a Creative Writing Competition. Get the media involved."

At the word "Media" my stomach clenched. I remember last time I wanted to involve the media in a project I had done with the students of the college. The PR woman Sabrina had not been... helpful.

I had been trying to raise money for terminally ill boy called Dylan to send him to Disney land, and the students had made cakes to donate towards a Fundraiser Day. Nuneaton News were publishing a story about it and wanted to involve the U.C.W with a story about the students helping. A picture was asked for, and I went through all the proper routes. But it was a brick wall as soon as I had approached Sabrina. She was the ultimate power-tripper.

You could tell she enjoyed having power over other people, enjoyed asserting her authority, enjoyed making people feel small and stupid. I had told the story to uncaring ears, sharing the little boy's plight with someone who literally could not give one flying toss about him. But she made all the right head gestures, nods and mmmms, but the smile never reached her eyes. The worst thing was, she gave me permission, and a form for the students to sign.

I went back up to class, rejoicing and excited, for her to interrupt the lesson, tell me she wasn't happy with the information she had given me and that I was not to mention anything about the College in the newspaper. My mouth was wide open in shock, and the students were appalled also.

"You can come back to me when you have more information," she said haughtily, her cream suit unblemished and perfect.

"But I've given you all the information I have," I said numbly. "The paper needs the story by tonight-"

"Well, no they don't really, do they?" she said, cocking her head to the side.

I was so shocked I couldn't even say anything. I walked away from her and back to my seat next to my learner, the white form of permission in front of me.

A minute later, she returned, walking into the class and snatched the form from in front of me. "You won't be needing that now, will you?" she said and walked away.

It was something that had always put a sour taste in my mouth whenever I heard her name. Sabrina Whitehead.

A renowned Prom Queen of Nuneaton with a long line of successful sisters who had also gained the title of Carnival Queen. She was the yearly judge of the future Carnival Queens and was always a guest at the major Nuneaton events. Now, I don't know whether I was just envious that I had never had a crown on my head or what- but I was pretty sure that my encounter with her decided that we wouldn't get along.

I had decided after that that I would always approach the papers alone if I was ever to do something again. I would never ask for her approval ever again. Things never got done unless you did them yourself.

A week passed and I had managed to clinch a deal with Nuneaton Academy about teaching a six week Creative Writing course at their school. I was mightily pleased and bought some salmon chunks for Ben as a celebration.

As a past student of Nuneaton Academy, I wondered what it would be like to return. I had been there for an interview in the past and couldn't get over how much it had changed. What had used to be considered as the worst school in Nuneaton was now one of the most successful. The uniform, the new builds and the new opportunities that were given to the students seemed to make up for all the crap it had put my generation through.

I just hoped there wouldn't be another Ellie Blackwell in there, struggling, bullied and despairing.

The college was also setting the way clear for this Creative Writing competition and I had walked past the first posters about it earlier that day.

"Things aren't going so badly, are they, Ben?" As usual he wouldn't answer. I rolled my eyes and tried again. "Things aren't going so bad, are they *Benedict?*"

He managed just to lift his head from the bowl of tuna to say, "Indeed!" before throwing his face back into it.

It was a weekend and I cracked open a bottle of wine. I had to admit, things had been getting better since Ben had come along. Work was progressing, and if Ben had never had come along to the library, then Jeff would never have started talking to me and agreed about the Creative Writing Course. He always answered my emails now and his wife had even come into work specially to see Ben.

Things started to clear and rationality crept in. The narrowed glances from the women in the office I had once seen as wary, were now the looks of exhausted colleagues. The murmuring between them, which I thought was about me, was now heard as discussions about students' needs.

My body stopped shaking, and for the first time, I could breathe.

Ben was a usual attraction at the college, but sometimes he didn't come along if he didn't want to. Sometimes he would make a mess of the house, so I would have to clean it up.

One day I had come back and he had knocked over my books and photo albums.

"For God's sake, Ben!" I snarled, picking up the precious pictures. Yeah- I hadn't looked at them for years, but it didn't stop them meaning any less to me. Annoyingly, he had knocked over a box of photographs that I hadn't managed to put properly into an album.

"It's all right for you," I carried on. "You don't have to do any cleaning or working or anything- you just sit there and lick your balls."

I looked up apologetically then, sensing it was a sore subject. "Oh, err- sorry about that."

He flicked his tail at me and set to licking himself.

I sighed as I started to pick up the pictures and came across a Tamworth album. Curiously, I opened it up- probably because it would put off me actually tidying. The first picture was of me and my sister watering plants together. We always loved doing that in the summer, filling up the watering cans and then filled up the parched mouths of flowers.

The next picture was of us again at Drayton Manor Zoo at the Rhino Enclosure. The next photo stopped me in my tracks. It was one of Ben.

I looked up at him. He was still a spitting image, and I wondered again how he had come to me. He never answered my questions when I asked him, never responded when I demanded how he had come back after all these years, how he could possibly still be alive, and most of all- how could he talk?

He would only ever say, "Can you just accept it for what it is?"

I would mutter something under my breath. Even bribery through catnip wouldn't work.

"See this? This is you."

Ben sniffed at it disinterestedly.

I leant back on my feet and put it aside, promising to frame it. The next photo brought a different reaction. "I thought I had gotten rid of all of these." That was a lie. I had never the heart to get rid of the photos. I had always hidden them, hoping I wouldn't find them again for years, only to hide them again if I did.

I'm talking about Barry.

It was a picture of a dark haired man with a little girl wearing a mini mouse top and a motorbike helmet, too big for her six year old head.

The little girl was me.

To my shame, I burst into tears. Ben was in my lap immediately, sitting on the picture away from my sight. He didn't say anything, but the pale orange of his eyes warmed me. Soon his sandpaper tongue was licking the salt tracks from my face.

"Sorry," I sniffed, realising that I was saying it to him for more than one reason. "I'm sorry for all of those things that happened, Ben."

He didn't say anything but began to purr.

We were silent that night, quietly enjoying each other's company until I felt myself falling asleep on the sofa. He curled up beside me and said, "Sleep, silly human."

And I did.

Chapter Four

The weekend came and went, with a strange visit from my mum. She continuously stared at Ben, saying that she couldn't believe how much he looked like him. Little did she know that it was actually the one and only.

Monday was not an enjoyable experience.

"You're going to have to put the media story through Sabrina, I'm afraid, Ellie," Jeff said to me.

"But, I'm supposed to be sending everything to the media tonight!"

Jeff shook his head. The Catering Department got into trouble because they put their competition through the media without the PR's approval-"

"Only because she was so slow into responding and didn't bring any coverage to the last event they did," I argued.

"Nevertheless, The Principal has caught wind of the competition, and she's notified me that she expects everything to go through the proper channels. Agreed?"

I would have loved to mutter something, but I was far too grown up for that, (stupid principal) and took a deep breath instead.

"Fine," I said. "But if she refuses to put it through, then I'm going to do it off my own back."

The next morning, I got up early even though it was my day off. I was going to go to the PR office armed and ready. Sabrina hadn't seen me since June and I had changed a lot. I was a newbie still then. Things had changed. I had grown in confidence, had discovered more about the business and had prepared for bitch-attack-number-one.

"Why are you getting so scrubbed up?" Ben asked, whilst looking up at me stretching on his back.

"Because," I said putting on my mascara, "a woman arms herself with makeup and posh clothes to kick arse."

"Why don't you just mark your territory?"

"I'm not pissing around her office, Ben."

"Works for me."

I arranged a portfolio of all of the relevant information, provided emails from other members of staff backing up the competition, the sponsors, the prizes, images of the website and posters advertising the event, as well as a drafted press release, which I knew she would throw away. She liked to write all of the U.C.W's press releases- but I wasn't giving her any opportunity to say no to me.

I knew I was being sneaky, but I was also going to be putting my phone on record to tape our conversation. I wasn't giving her any chance to talk to me the way she did last time without proof.

I wondered if she would recognise me. I doubt she would. People like her don't remember the inferior.

I walked there determinedly with Ben at my side. The whiskers and milk were waiting for him as always. He had put on some much needed weight since he had been living with me, and it was a relief to see him as I always thought he should look. He had stopped scratching around his ears due to the cream the vets had given me, had been wormed, inoculated and everything else a cat could wish for.

He meowed loudly at me as I walked in, but it was a good-luck meow.

Sabrina's office was pretty much nestled a few steps away from reception, right next to the Principal's, which of course I'm sure she prided herself on.

I knocked on the door, making sure I had my name badge in clear view. I had it changed in October when I had become a Sessional Lecturer. For some reason I thought it looked better than having "Teaching Assistant" on there.

There wasn't an answer so I opened it anyway. Sabrina was sitting at her desk, long red hair tied back and a perfect fitted cream suit on. I half wondered if it was the one that she had worn when she had humiliated me in front of my students.

I straightened up, knowing that I looked good. I had curled my blonde hair and pinned it up, wore a knee length pencil skirt and a green top with burgundy blazer. Too sensible for heels, I had polished my flat knee high leather boots instead.

Fixing my best professional smile on, I walked in, pressing the button on my phone to *record* as I did.

"Hi, my name is Ellena Blackwell. I've come here to talk to you about doing a press release."

Her brown eyes ran up and down me. I don't think she recognised me but she stopped typing.

"Ok, go on," she said, not offering me a seat.

"We've set up a Creative Writing Competition for the college students," I said. "We've generated a lot of interest and I don't know if you've seen, but we've had posters put around the college for it."

"I have seen," she said, her smile cold.

"I wanted to put the story in The Nuneaton News," I continued. "I have great links with the reporters there who did some coverage of an event I did awhile back, and I think the extra coverage would be brilliant. I hope to get a story up about the event before it officially opens for entries, and one for when the winner is announced."

"Right..." Sabrina looked back to her screen and did a few clicks away from an email she was on. Her skin was a perfect cream colour that would never suit a fake tan. Her fingers long and nails painted a conservative pink colour, her ring finger holding a huge diamond.

Another thing to envy.

Not waiting to be asked, I pointedly took off my jacket and sat in front of her. "I have the Director of Foundation Learning who is backing the event, as well as the Manager of Student Services. I have a folder here containing all of the relevant information."

She took the folder I had in my hands and put it in front of her. "I will have to look into this properly..." she said, a fake smile leaking the corners of her face.

"Wonderful," I said. "The event officially opens next week. I have already contacted the Newspapers and they said they would like to get the story in for this week."

"The reporters always say that," Sabrina started.

"It is vital to get this story out as early as possible."

Her eyes narrowed. "I don't believe the U.C.W caters to Creative Writing, is that true?"

"It doesn't, but hopefully maybe in the future, it will. This competition is the start." I was glad that my voice was clear, calm brooking no argument. This was her job. There was no reason why she couldn't help me. "I was also hoping for the college to donate money towards the prizes? Nothing too over the top. Maybe some tickets to Drayton Manor or Gift Vouchers?"

Sabrina took a breath and folded her hands on the desk in front of her. "I don't know if you have realised or read your emails, but the College Funds are tight, and we don't have the excess to support competitions towards subjects the college doesn't even support."

I was ready for this. "If that is the case," I said calmly, "then maybe the U.C.W can offer free services, such as gift vouchers for the beauty salon upstairs or a free meal at the college restaurant? Maybe even flowers from the floristry department?" I smiled my reasonable smile.

Sabrina picked up my folder and put it in one of her office drawers. "We will see what we can do."

I stared at her, wondering how old she was and if we had anything in common. She appeared the same age as me- but I knew already that we were on different worlds. The only thing that made us possibly similar was the small tattoo on her wrist (I have three).

"Is there any chance we can get a press release sorted for the papers this week?" I asked, snapping my eyes away from it.

"Well, I'll see what I can do," she sighed, a slight Yorkshire accent poking through, making me blink in surprise. "I will have to read all of the information and make sure that this event is actually going through."

Alarm bells rang for some reason. "It is definitely going through," I said. "We've got posters up- set up a page on the website about it. The students are excited."

"But that comes at an unnecessary expense, seeing that we don't even support that subject here." She sighed again. "And if you also check your emails, you will see that we are expecting a visit from His Royal Highness, the Duke of Edinburgh. Every penny will be going towards making that event as high quality as possible. I'm afraid a lot of my time will be spent arranging press releases for that. You can understand how that is my priority."

"So will the press release be prepared for this week?"

She puffed air from her perfectly blushed cheeks. "Who can say?" A small smile played at the corner of her lips, and I could see that she was enjoying seeing my sudden discomfort.

"How is the boy you did that charity event for anyway?" she asked, fake politeness inked into her voice.

I went cold. "He died."

"Shame."

I stood then and walked out.

I was halfway to Jeff's office before I realised that in my fury I had left my jacket there. I swore angrily, and went to go back.

"No, I'll look like a right idiot," I snarled, turning around again.

Jeff wasn't in his office, and I growled in annoyance, turning to the Library instead.

Fine. I would sort this out for myself. Things never worked when I was at the mercy of other people. I couldn't expect other people to make things happen for me- I would have to take control myself. Within half an hour, I had emailed three newspapers, two radio stations, and several online blogs the press release I had drafted about the event, including pictures and jpegs of the promotional posters.

This event was going to be a success, whether Sabrina wanted it to be or not.

Ben was there waiting for me as expected.

"Are you ok?" he meowed, sensing my mood. I shivered in the cold and shook my head.

"I've got to go back- I forgot my jacket."

"Go get it then."

I looked back towards reception and shook my head. "I can't- I left it in Sabrina's office and she's such a horrible person. I really hate her. I don't want to get it whilst she's in there."

A student walked out of the building and as the automatic doors opened, Ben darted in.

"Wait! Ben!"

I rushed in after him, but Janet the Student Support Manager stopped me. "Hi Ellie, how are you?"

"I'm really well thanks," I said, trying to crane my neck to see where Ben had gone.

"Just a quick one to let you know, I've spoken to Tracey about the Restart Programme and let her know you're interested."

"Oh thanks for that," I said, "I really appreciate it."

Janet walked away smiling, and I suddenly realised that it had been a genuine smile. When had that happened?

I was just about to walk down the hallway where Sabrina's office was, when I heard a huge shriek. Everyone in reception just about jumped out of their skin when Sabrina came storming out towards the reception desk, a yellow stain marring her perfect cream suit.

"I want security in my office right now!" she seethed. "There is a wild cat trashing the place, and I want him out now!"

"A wild cat?" the receptionist stammered.

"Yes, a wild cat!" Now do I have to call security, or are you going to do it?"

The young receptionist woman looked helplessly to her fellow colleagues. "We don't have security at the college-"

Before Sabrina started shouting even more, I ran down the hallway and into her office. Ben was there, busying spraying everywhere, my jacket thankfully unharmed in the process. I grabbed it and with a meow of surprise, I picked up Ben and wrapped him in it.

Walking out, I could hear Sabrina's rants coming closer.

Knowing there was no way to avoid her without walking straight into her I darted into the toilets opposite the offending office. I twisted the lock and heard her door open and slam shut.

Ben's pale ginger head peeked out and licked my chin.

"What did you *do*?" I breathed in disbelief.

"I created a diversion," he said simply, and not without pride.

"Is this you marking your territory?"

"It worked, didn't it?"

I didn't hide long in that toilet, afraid that she would want to come in and attempt to wash the cat piss from her suit.

"You stay quiet, ok?" I hissed, opening my bag. I was finally thankful of insisting carrying a huge tote bag with me.

"I'm not getting in that," he meowed.

"You bloody are," I said, unceremoniously shoving him in it.

Within 44 seconds, I had unbolted the door, was out of the reception and into the cold, Sabrina's snarls of destroying, "That filthy ginger cat" loud in my ears.

It was only when I was outside the gates when I started to laugh.

Ben got lots of cuddles that night, as we both recounted what happened and laughed about it. I didn't have work the next day, so me and Ben decided to have a night on the town- Ben to find whatever lady friends he wanted, and me, out with my friends at the Tav.

For the first time in a long time, I was feeling carefree. Things were going in the right direction, however weird and manic.

Yeah, my best friend was a talking cat, but I realised I was incredibly happy. It was like having a part of my past come back to me, maybe even a part of myself. Something to say- that time isn't forgotten. I was there too. And although we didn't talk about Tamworth,

Barry, or the things that were plaguing my mind, we took each day at a time. One day I would deal with that stuff, but at the moment, I was repairing my spirit.

The anniversary of my Granddad's death had come and gone, and Ben had come with me to the church yard, which my family was finding strange. I had argued that whereas they have their dogs to go with them everywhere, so did Ben. He wasn't too happy that I had compared him to a dog and wouldn't speak to me until I had promised to buy him a new catnip toy.

St Wilfred's was a place I went to simply to sit and talk to my Granddad, cousin and uncle. Sounds excessive? I suppose it was. A lot of needless deaths in our family. St Wilfred's was a place I cleared my head and started again.

"I get most of my answers from here, Ben," I said as I knelt by my Granddad's graveside. "Whenever I get the most desperate, I come here."

I didn't have to say anything to Ben about the way I felt. I think he knew. He was a silent pale orange present in a world of grey. My Granddad was my dad in so many ways. We grew up in his house, were there every weekend, every holiday, and moved in with him when we moved from Tamworth. He was everything- an inspiration. He was a male force that I wanted to be proud of me. I needed that space filled where Barry had walked out of- not that he had ever tried to contribute anything towards it. I suppose even now I am damaged from it. Always striving for approval. Always trying to push myself and achieve the most I can to make someone proud of me. Or maybe I was trying to convince myself I was someone worth to love.

When people talk about the end, they always describe it as a relief for old people. Movies depict it was a peaceful thing that happens with a sunset and birds flying over trees. It isn't. Cancer is an ugly, evil thing that chokes, twists and starves.

Every day is a dedication to him. Sometimes I forget he is gone. The most significant and amazing man in my life. Sometimes I felt as though I had no place to grieve for him as powerfully as his children. I was a grandchild. But he was my dad in so many ways, and I loved him so much.

Every day I prayed that he knew how much I loved him, and how sorry I was that I wasn't there at the end.

I sat there in the pub, surrounded by friends, envisioning a future ahead, and someone who would be at home waiting for me. Hey- it was my cat, but it counted for something.

I was getting a bit tipsy by the time I started ranting about the poor service from Public Relations at the college.

My friend, Emily gasped at the mention. "Public Relations?" she said. "At the college?"

"Yes, and yes," I said, nodding to both questions.

"I've had an interview for there last week!"

We both laughed and I said I pitied her. She was applying for the post of administration assistant in the department. I told her not to mention she knew me else she probably would get sacked- that's if she got the job. I half prayed for her own sake that she wouldn't.

I liked Emily. I hated the fact that men seemed to take advantage of her. I think she was a bit like me. She just wanted to be loved. I think when dads leave their daughters then they are left craving for some sort of love- somehow desperate to prove they are worthy of it. God knows I've been there.

But she was definitely a looker. The longest blonde hair I would love for her to cut into a bob, big model lips, always glossed a subtle pink or ravishing red and a natural beauty and innocence that made you just want to squeeze her.

I was glad that she was trying to get somewhere in her career. She worked at the Perfume Shop in town and every birthday present, although perfume, was always some gorgeous scent that I used until I ran out. She was one of the few in Nuneaton that constantly smelt good.

I went to the toilet whilst she got us some more drinks and I stared at my reflection as I washed my hands. My eyes are grey like Barry's- but I liked to say it was from my Nan's side of the family on my mother's side. My hair was blonde like my mother's (ok, it was dyed) and I was aiming for it to be long like my Granddad liked it. I didn't have a boyfriend- hadn't for a long time. I think I was just happy on my own- well, maybe I'm lying, but at the moment it was the only way I could be. I had to get myself sorted before I could be with anyone else. But sometimes guys just saw a pretty face and wouldn't try and delve deeper. That put me off trusting a lot of them.

I returned to the table and enjoyed spending time with my friends. I didn't want to dwell on everything that had happened in the past- because it was exactly that- the past. I was in charge of creating my future.

I came back home rather pissed that night... ok early morning.

Ben was sitting there, his face sniffing the new catnip toy I had gotten him. I cackled as soon as I got in, kicking off my shoes and crawling my way to the sofa.

"Aren't we a pair?" I said reaching for him and pulling him to my chest. His purring tickled my cheek and I giggled. "I don't know why you came back, or how," I said, "but I'm glad and love you lots and lot and jelly tots."

Ben licked my face.

"That is the most ridiculous thing I have ever heard," he said. "But I love you too, my silly human"

I sat numbly shoving cornflakes into my mouth the next morning, looking through photos of last night on my phone, moaning at the ones I was dancing around a pole with Emily.

It was snowing today, so we were stuck in the house- not that we minded. I had the heating on full blast after just topping up my gas card and there was a lovely selection of Disney films for us to watch that afternoon. I had the Lion King out, thinking it may appeal to him, seeing how he hated Beauty and the Beast so much.

Mum had texted me saying my sister Kayleigh had gone into labour. I was anxious and constantly checking up via text to my brother in law. I tried to distract myself by going through my photographs; I then remembered the recording in Sabrina's office.

"Hey Ben," I shouted to the kitchen, knowing he currently had his face stuck into a bowl of Whiskers

Finest, "do you want to listen to this conversation with Sabrina?" He didn't answer. "It'll have the sounds of her shrieking when you peed on her!"

Within a second, he came in, licking his chops.

"I may be curious to hear this," he said, jumping onto the table next to my cornflakes.

I clicked onto the recording as he started to lap up the rest of my cereal's milk.

Sure enough, our conversation played out. I cringed at some parts and giggled at others.

"We'll have to wait for a bit when I leave the office, because I was in the library for a while," I said.

"What was all that about?"

"Oh just some teaching assistant who wants a press release for a competition."

I bristled at that. My badge said Sessional Lecturer!

"Right. Have you sorted out the accounts?"

"All done."

"Good. This divorce is going to cost me. I'm not letting him have the farmhouse in Stratford."

"Why would he want that?"

"Apparently his new bitch loves horses. I'd rather pull down my inheritance brick by brick, tree by tree than have her house her stupid ponies in there."

An awkward silence.

"Have you booked those flights?"

"Yes, confirmed, first class."

"Good. What about the money transfer?"

"It'll be in your account next Monday. It's under safety procedures and various trainee sessions."

A tittering of too high pitched laughter made Ben flinch. "Fabulous. What about the exchange? Has your fiancé sorted out that as well? I'm investing a lot of money in him, Sabrina.

"I understand that, Principal, but Rino is subtle and had been in the business for years. He has a lot of contacts overseas."

"Good. I will say, Sabrina, I didn't expect you to be marrying a drug dealer like him."

"I didn't expect you to be a money swindler either, Principal."

A pause went past and then they cackled, sharing in some sort of hilarious joke.

"How much money have we projected to spend on the new building?"

"It was going to be half a million, but the surveyor says he can draw up the quote for twice that."

"Wonderful. Forty percent towards your new house in Marbella, and sixty towards mine in Malibu."

"The draft won't be ready till the summer however," Sabrina's voice drawled.

"What a shame. Anyway, I have a meeting with the Council about more funding, will you have my driver come pick me up for the airport next week?"

"Already done, Principal."

"And when are the new filing cabinets coming?"

"Same day as interviews."

"Perfect."

The sound of a door opening and shutting followed, along with a phone call with the Payroll Department, and then silence.

A knock on the door. *"Hello, Sabrina, can we-"*

"Oh my God!"

A chorus of shrieks, meows hisses came, mixed with swearing, something smashing and a door slamming.

I couldn't listen to anymore.

"Oh my God..." I breathed.

"I know- can you believe what she called me?!"

"Sabrina and the Principal are running a scam!"

Chapter Five

It was difficult thinking about the next few moments. What was I supposed to do? Should I call the police? Should I confront them? The next day, I decided to do the right thing.

I went to the police station and told them everything.

"That is a very serious allegation to make, miss," one of the constables said. I shifted uncomfortably under his dark brown gaze. "Hey- is that your cat outside?"

I was asked to come into another room by a larger and older man. He had a wide face, open, welcoming, but tired also. His hair was grey but he had a thick head of it. I wondered how long he had been in the business, but dare not even ask. I didn't want to get into one of those conversations about the horrors he had seen.

I played the recording to him in a small clinical room. I didn't like the man who escorted me. He was tall, and yes, actually quite handsome, but there was something in his steel chipped gaze reeking of suspicion. I didn't trust people who were suspicious of me. I could tell he wanted to sit in on our conversation, but was relieved when the door shut in front of him.

The older policeman, named Jake O'Hara, listened gravely to it, all of it, even to the very last meow.

To my surprise it had even finished before Ben had started talking to me. I hadn't even thought of that.

"This is very serious," he said. "A serious allegation."

"Well, I wouldn't come here unless I thought it was so," I said, putting my phone back in my pocket.

"There's not much we can do without evidence," he said then, dashing my hopes.

"I thought that was evidence?" a scowl covered my face.

"It's not hard evidence," he laughed at me. "That could be a recording of anything- a television program. There's nothing specific in it. You could have even made it up."

"But I didn't!" I exclaimed, affronted.

He laughed at me again- I didn't like that. "Look, I can go down there with an enquiry, but other than that, there's not much I can do."

I stared at him, shocked, appalled and embarrassed. "So I've come here for no reason?"

"No, of course not," he chided me as if I was stupid. "It's always good to come to the police if you fear something illegal is going on."

"But it *is* going on!"

He laughed at me again, and I decided there and then that I didn't like this man. "Like I say, I can go down there and make enquiries. But I wouldn't go shouting this about. You could lose your job over this."

Something in me then, told me that this wasn't what a policeman should be saying to a young woman. Maybe I came across as vulnerable, but I wasn't. I played on it anyways.

"You really think so?" I said in my best fragile voice. "I don't want that to happen. I love my job."

"Best to stay quiet about it then, lass, ok?"

"Ok," I said, looking down at my phone. "Maybe I should just delete the recording? Forget it ever happened?"

His fat hands covered mine, peppered with broken veins and dry skin. "Best to do that, love," he soothed, his pink tongue fat and treacherous in his too wet mouth. "Delete it and forget it happened."

I pressed *delete* then, sending the recording into oblivion.

"Good lass. You know it makes sense."

Furious that he would use one of my favourite quotes by one of my most loved actors, I put my best sad smile face on and nodded.

"Maybe you're right."

I left the room with the inspector giving me his card, the paper small in his chubby fingers. He walked off then, dealing with something he probably deemed more important.

The man who escorted me, wearing his dark grey suit and thin black tie stared at me as I signed out. He walked over to me, dark stubble marking an arrogant chin.

"Can I have a word?" he asked.

I raised my eyebrow at him and then looked out the door. Ben was jumping in and out of the snow. I'm not sure if he had seen it this deep before, but he was making an absolute fool of himself, much to the children's delight.

"About?" I had already decided I didn't like policemen from this department and I definitely wasn't going to like him, if that inspector was someone he was working for.

He looked annoyed then, as if I was being awkward. "Here's my card," he said, getting one out from inside his jacket. I glanced at it.

Detective Arthur Calloway

0773980202

I raised my eyebrows at the name.

"Thanks," I said, not meaning it.

"Calloway, there's a call for you on Line Three-," said the receptionist suddenly, the drunk still singing in the background.

"Can he hold for a second?" Arthur demanded, his dark green eyes narrowing in annoyance.

"It's Detective Avery from Stratford," pressed the receptionist sheepishly.

Arthur rolled his eyes. "Wait here for a second?"

I watched him walk away to take the call and didn't waste any time. I walked out of the doors and into the snow, calling Ben as I went.

I know the detective may have been smug, expecting to see my name on the register as I signed in and out.

But all he would see would be a big X.

My priority when I got home was to get Ben warm. He let me carry him the rest of the way home, even though he had enjoyed the snow.

"What are you going to do now?" he asked me.

"I don't know," I said. "But I'm uploading the recording straight back onto my phone, that's for sure!"

That police officer must have thought I was really stupid. As if I would delete something like that. I had saved that file to my Google docs, a USB and a cd. But what else could you do if the police wouldn't actually help you?

Emily called me later on that day to say she had gotten an email saying that she had a second interview and would I like to meet her afterwards. I said yes, thinking I could do with the distraction.

How far do you go to do what's right? I felt completely alone in this- besides from Ben, of course. But he thought a bit of catnip could set anything right. I did try having a sniff of it when he offered, but it didn't do anything for me.

One good thing that happened that night- my sister had a baby. My mother called me at two o'clock in the morning letting me know the good news. I wouldn't be able to see her until visiting hours the next day however and for a moment, I forgot the worries of college.

The baby was 10lbs3 and delivered by C-section. I was so excited, I couldn't wait. I even woke up Ben to tell him, but I don't think he was that fussed.

The next morning I was called by work to let me know that my student wouldn't be in. I didn't mind too much. I decided that Sabrina could wait whilst I saw my sister in hospital.

I turned up with my mother in the thick of snow to see this huge baby, which they had named Rowan. I burst into tears when I saw him. It was as if everything bad that had happened over the year could be officially forgiven and forgotten about. This was the new beginning. When I held him for the first time I was terrified. He was so heavy and after a while, I was keen to pass the responsibility over to my mother.

Rowan was truly beautiful and my sister had done so well. She was exhausted and so was Ryan, her husband.

I went home, happy and bubbling with news to tell Ben. I then realised that I hadn't even told Emily that I wouldn't be able to meet her after her interview. I checked my phone and saw that there were no messages or missed calls.

I texted her apologising and explaining what had happened, and said that I hoped her interview had gone well.

Later on that night when I logged into my Facebook account, something disturbing had been posted by Emily's sister.

11:32pm: No one can get in contact with Emily. Can someone please let us know where she is?

I logged in again in the middle of the night when I went to the toilet.

It was from Emily's housemate this time.

04:03am *We're really worried- if anyone is with Emily, can they let us know she's ok?xxx*

I fell back to sleep, nightmares plaguing me of Sabrina's laughing face.

The next day as I logged into my emails, Ben shovelled his face into another bowl of whiskers. I had read more disturbing pleas of information from my friends on Facebook about Emily, and that she hadn't been seen all day since she had set off for her 2nd interview.

I almost dropped my tea at the sight of my emails.

Dear Miss Blackwell,

Your presence is requested at soonest convenience, as a reference to Miss Emily Baker for the position of Administrator.

Regards,

Sabrina Whitehead

Public Relations Officer to Principal

University College of Warwickshire

Oh God, she put me as a reference? Why the hell would she do that?

I pulled out the cards the police officers had given me. One with Jake O'Hara, and the other with Arthur Calloway. They weren't going to help me. One encouraged me to destroy a vital piece of evidence, and the other was intimidating as hell, and worked in the same department as the first idiot.

"What do you think, Ben?" I asked.

He walked is, licking his paws clean from tuna whiskers. "Mark your territory?"

"Too right."

I dressed for battle the next day and refused to go and see Sabrina until my lessons were over. I knocked on the door, flicking my phone to record again.

She was dressed in a black suit this time, her eyes narrowed and skin looking dry.

"Please, take a seat," she said, gesturing the chair before her desk.

I sat in it, surprised.

"We had an interviewee come in the other day, by the name of Emily Baker, and she put you as a reference."

There was something in her voice that made my skin prickle. Something in her smile that looked sadistic. I looked down at her hands that were twitching across her keyboard. Saw scratches.

"We were very interested in what Emily had to say about your relationship," she continued. "She led us to believe that you are a very valued friend."

"And?" I said my voice dry.

"Well, we would take it for granted you would hold Emily in the same regard as she has you."

I was silent, until I suddenly realised that I wasn't alone in the room. A man walked out of the Principal's office, good looking and dark. Intuition told me he was her boyfriend.

"Rino, I take it?" I asked snidely.

Rowena stood, locked the office door and drew the blinds shut.

Panic grabbed me for one second and I stood until heavy hands shoved me back down.

"Make one move, and I'll rag that pretty hair from your scalp," he promised sweetly in my ear.

"Get her bag," Sabrina instructed.

To my dismay, Rino grabbed my handbag and emptied the contents onto her desk, until my lovely phone full of pictures of Rowan fell out.

Sabrina opened a drawer and pulled out a hammer. "Do you think you can fuck with me, you stupid TA?" she sneered in my face.

"Actually, I'm a Sessional Lecturer."

She scowled at me and whacked the hammer down full force onto my phone, the screen smashing into bits. She then threw it to Rino, who started stamping on it.

"Now you're going to stay quiet, aren't you?" she hissed, spitting on my face as she shoved the hammer beneath my chin. "Else each one of your precious friend's fingers are going to get snapped, crushed and sent back to you."

"And when are you thinking of letting her go?" I dared to ask, terrified but adrenaline making my tongue stupid. "When you finally retire from here?"

"Our retirement is coming faster than you think!"

"Why don't we just take her now?" said Rino. "Put her with the other girl?"

Sabrina looked thoughtful, which terrified me most of all. "Well actually, "I said. "If you do decide to do that then you're fucked either way."

Rino grabbed my hair and yanked my head back. "What are you on about?"

"Do you think I'm the only person who knows about the recording?" My bullshit meter hit the roof and an Oscar winning actor's performance sprang forth. "Do you think I would be so stupid to just have it on my phone? I have it on USBs, CDs and have even got it blue-toothed onto my mate's phone! He knows about this meeting! He was listening all the time on the other end of the phone before you smashed it up- if anything happens to me, he'll upload the clip to YouTube and spread it faster than a fart at a wedding!"

Sabrina's face couldn't have been paler. She nodded to Rino, and he suddenly let me go.

She pointed the hammer at me, hand shaking. "You best get all of those recordings and deliver them to us. If anything gets leaked out, you and your friend are dead. You hear me? *Dead!*"

I stood up then and was just about hauled to my tiptoes by Rino. "She's serious, blondie. And so am I."

I flinched at his whiskey smelling breath and tried to pull away from him.

"You've got yourself mucked in with some very bad people, you know that?" he growled. "I know people who will hunt you down and pull apart every member of your family limb by limb." He grinned then, revealing a gold tooth. "They get off on it sweetheart. And so do I." He threw me away then as if I was a bag of rubbish.

I had no doubt someone was following me home on the way back. My legs were wobbling with each step I took, my breath ragged in my chest. I wanted to lose them before I got to the flat. My flat wasn't registered at the U.C.W, but my parents' house was. I hated the thought of anything happening to them, especially my sister and little Rowan. I needed help.

Ben walked loyally by my side. He knew we were being pursued, and I started following Ben down small lanes and little pathways over bridges and back again. We were leading the man behind us on a goose chase. Soon, it started to snow, and we couldn't keep it up for much longer.

Ben jumped up into my coat and I cuddled him close to my chest as he meowed directions to me. It started to get dark then and I was truly getting scared.

I chanced looking behind and saw that the one man had turned into two. I knew they were following me for my address. Knew as soon as they found it that was it. I couldn't see their features because of the weather, just that they were wearing heavy coats. But I noticed they had started to slip and skid in the white that had started to settle.

My boots had been regripped recently and were excellent walking through snow. It started to fall heavier and my feet began to walk faster.

"Time to run, Ellena!" meowed Ben, diving from my chest and leading the way. I broke out into a fast sprint, choosing to run across the grass instead of the pavement, knowing from previous walks that it was packed with ice. I heard a shout, a loud noise and didn't have to turn around to know one of them had slipped.

I blessed the day Ben was born ginger, as I could just make out the sight of his coat through the white substance falling around me. He darted down an alleyway and I followed, up into an estate, through some trees and down another alleyway.

Adrenaline pumped breath into my lungs as I soon realised we were running up a hill towards the old train tracks. I looked back and could see one looming shadow behind.

"Follow me!" Ben howled. My chest was burning now, the cold air freezing the hot blood pumping into those precious organs.

I looked back again and saw nothing but white.

"They're gone, Ben!" I rasped, trying to keep up. We ran over a bridge and went under it. I paused then, exhausted and rested my hands on my thighs. "God- I'm so-"

A scream was strangled out of me then when a freezing hand covered my mouth. I fell against a warm body as it dragged me further beneath the tunnel and pinned me against the wall.

Arthur Calloway's face radiated heat against mine it was so close. He held a finger to his lips, and then pointing upwards.

Confusion raged in my head until I heard two thick accents.

"She's gone!"

"Oh, well done, numb nuts!" the other growled. "I can see that!"

"It's your fault falling over like a fucking idiot."

"How did I know it was going to snow?" A moaning followed then. "I think I've sprained my ankle- come on, let's just tell the boss and his missus we've lost her."

"We can tell them *you* lost her if you like!"

"You are a right cheeky git..."

The voices became fainter, and Calloway's hand warmed against my mouth. It was only when we were surrounded by silence when he finally stepped away. I realised however that he still had not released his hold on my arm.

"I think we need to talk," he said.

Chapter Six

The inside of Calloway's car was much welcome when me and Ben got to it.

"No- the cat stays outside," he said, waving his head and shaking his head.

"If you want to talk to me, you'll have to talk to my cat as well," I growled, one foot already in the vehicle. I must have looked like a mad woman, standing there covered in snow with a shivering ginger ball in my arms. The detective scowled and then jutted his head to motion me to get in.

Calloway drove for a while until he was sure no one was following us and pulled into a random country pub car park. The pub was boarded up and forgotten, deserted and destitute. It was a depressing sight.

"You've been following me," I said, rubbing life back into Ben's cold ears.

"So were those men," he answered, frowning at the wet moggy in his car. "Any idea why?"

A few, I thought. Should I tell him about everything? I bit my lip. "How do you get on with Jake O'Hara?"

I was rewarded by a surprised blink. "The man's a cock."

That was my cue.

I told him everything. Right from the beginning, the recording, the interview with O'Hara, to him urging me to deleting it, to Emily going missing, the threats from Rino and Sabrina to my shoe size, how I liked my tea and my star sign. I told him everything.

"He told you to delete a piece of evidence?" Calloway said, his jaw locking in anger.

"Yeah, I deleted it in front of him. I think he must have connections with the Principle, because Sabrina demanded my phone and smashed it up."

Calloway paled then and rubbed his forehead. "Are you telling me," he said in the voice of a man that had spent too much time and energy in searching for me as it is, "that after everything, you deleted the evidence?"

"I'm not stupid!" I snapped. "I have it backed up at my flat on USB, my laptop and on a CD."

He raised his eyebrows at me, surprised.

"What can I say?" I said with an embarrassed shrug. "I love detective films." A thought occurred to me then. "Why did you follow me?"

Calloway looked uncomfortable then, as if unsure on how much she should disclose to me. "We've had an investigation into Detective O'Hara for a while, of abusing the system. We've never had enough evidence to support anything however. When I checked the tapes to watch your interview with him, I saw that there weren't any. I became suspicious and started digging around."

"That still doesn't explain how you found me."

"Girl with a ginger cat who follows her everywhere? Including walking her to and from work?" he said looking smug. "I think that makes you very easy to track down. Your cat has his own Facebook page."

"But how did you- he has *whaaat*-?"

"Your Principal has been done before about scamming the system out of money. Constant trips to Hong Kong to see the school twinned with the U.C.W. Always flies first class. Always goes for a fortnight. Stays in the top hotels."

My head was buzzing. Ben's purring brought me back to earth before I had a panic attack.

"So why can't you just arrest them now and be done with it?"

He shook his head. "O'Hara and the Principal Jennifer Bowers have a lot of friends in high places-especially within the justice system," he said. "We need to collect so much evidence that they will choke on it. Plus," he added, "They have your friend Emily. Seems like discretion is in order. One false move-"

That did me there and then. I burst into tears in that car. I don't know how long I cried for, but I clung onto Ben like a lifeline.

"Oh God," I sobbed. "Oh God, oh God, oh *God!*"

"I suppose that means you're not up for the next part of the plan then?" Calloway said, awkwardly patting me on the back.

"What's that?" I said, wiping snot from my nose.

"We need you to go back into Sabrina's office." He threw a paper in my lap, the front page confirming a sudden fear. I had no choice but to send these bastards down.

Detectives Hunt for Missing Woman.

A picture of Emily's face smiled on the front, oblivious to the troubles what being my friend could do.

I didn't dare log onto Facebook when I got home that night. I couldn't read the pleas of her family and friends when I knew what had happened to her.

I hated to think what they were doing to her- how scared she was. That I was responsible...

"You can sleep on the sofa," I said to Calloway as he shuffled into my flat.

I don't think Ben liked him being there, but he didn't say anything- well, he couldn't anyway. He just pointedly walked to the kitchen and meowed at his bowl. I rolled my eyes and fed him some Whiskers.

Calloway had insisted on staying the night. I didn't know if that was protocol- maybe it wasn't, but I could tell for whatever reason he really wanted O'Hara. I would be lying if I didn't feel a bit safer knowing that he was in the next room.

"Feel free to use whatever facilities you need," I said. When he didn't answer and just nodded at me, I turned away and went into my room. I wasted an hour getting ready for bed, painted my toenails and brushed out Ben's coat.

"You ok?" I asked him quietly.

"Yes," he said. "But I don't like him being here. He smells of dog."

I raised my eyebrows at him and laughed. Stopping myself suddenly, I stood up and put my ear to the door. I could hear him talking. I opened it slightly and saw him pacing around the living room, hissing on the phone.

"We can't ask her to do that, it's too dangerous!" he snarled. "She's agreed to go into the PR woman's office and that's about as far as I'm willing to go with it... I don't care if it gets results! We have a missing person and another under threat." He turned then, saw me and quickly shut off his phone.

I opened the door wider, wondering if I could get away with not eavesdropping. "Who was that?" I asked.

"People higher up," he said simply.

"They want me to do what?"

"It doesn't matter," he snapped. "What matters is that we get tomorrow straight."

"What do you need from Sabrina's office anyway?"

"Files," he said. "We believe she may have documents about the Principal's expenses or her own. Maybe emails between business associates?"

I frowned. "Why can't you just seize the computers?"

He smiled as if he was talking to a child. "Because if I send a team out there to the college, O'Hara will get wind of it and the documents will be destroyed." He took a breath and put his hands on his hips. "Unfortunately, even the Justice System is corrupt."

"Are you?"

He stared at me. "I'm one of the few people you can trust, Ellena."

His words repeating in my head, I went to bed with an uneasy mind. He wouldn't tell me what could be done about Emily. That familiar feeling of panic was rising up. I Skyped my dad, and I'm sure Calloway was eavesdropping from the other side of the door to make sure I didn't give anything away.

Luckily, I had just about the right amount of adrenaline left to talk about Kayleigh's baby and hopefully coming over to see him in the Summer. My dad told me he was missing my mum and couldn't wait to see her in the next week or so. My mother was living back at the house with Kayleigh and Ryan coinciding somewhat uncomfortably. They were keen to start their lives together with the baby, and I think they probably didn't want to bicker in front of my mum, much to her amusement.

I fell asleep exhausted; Ben curled up under the covers with me against my tummy. I don't know why, but I suddenly felt a sense of peace being there with my oldest friend. Say what you like- but he stood for all of those moments I would sit on the pavement in Tamworth upset, lonely, angry and happy, content to sit on my lap and purr or lie in the sun with me.

He was my childhood lying right next to me.

I was dreaming. My Granddad was sitting in his chair in front of me, Ben in his lap. He was in my Nan's front room, in his favourite cardigan.

"Granddad?" I forgot then that he was gone. It was all a mistake. He was still here. I could tell the family. They would be so happy.

"Someone's looking after you here," he said, tickling the scruff of Ben, who in his half-closed eyed state was in bliss. He looked at me with his pale blue eyes that my Nan would always tell me used to be green.

I was holding his hand. His hands were huge, dotted with freckles and age spots. I loved his hands. Their constant strength.

Then I heard what I have always craved to hear from him. "You're a good Granddaughter, Ellena."

"Wake up," Ben meowed.

"Yes," my Granddad said, smiling again, giving Ben a squeeze. "Time to wake up."

A smashing sound woke me up with a bolt, my Granddad sinking from view.

"Granddad?!" I shouted, jumping to my feet.

I then realised where I was, who I was and that I still had a talking cat.

"It's coming from the lounge!" Ben hissed.

"Stay here!" I whispered, opening the door.

Grunts were coming from the dark with the added sound of something hard hitting flesh.

Instinct told me to grab something, and my hands found something solid.

My hand ran along the wall, seeing two shadows tussling on the floor. I flicked on the light just in time to see a man give a hard kick to Calloway's ribs. Health and safety suddenly having no meaning, I leapt across the broken ceramics on the floor, feeling an unfamiliar aggression building in my chest. With a growl, I hit the man as hard as I could with my weapon. He turned just in time to see a bottle of Jack Daniels BBQ sauce smash onto his head, before collapsing in a gurgled heap.

I stood there frozen as Calloway coughed and groaned. My house was a mess. Debris lay everywhere, a chair was overturned and a basket of washing had fallen from the table. I looked at the detective, spots of blood marring his white shirt.

"Give me a hand, would you?" he wheezed clutching his ribs.

I looked around at the broken pottery on the floor, aghast. "Did you smash my cat-lamp?"

"Your *what*?"

"My cat-lamp!" I picked up the broken black head of a cat, the build and shade shattered. "Oh great," I said dropping it. "Why didn't you just smash up my soul why don't you?" I turned to the intruder and kicked him in the ribs. "Why don't you just fuck-up-my-life-then-why-don't-you!" I snarled between kicks.

Finally, hands hauled me away from the thug.

"Calm down!" Calloway pulled out some handcuffs and set about securing the idiot.

"I should have kicked him in the balls."

The detective said nothing, but left the room to make a call. Whilst he was gone I made myself busy. I heard the soft drone of his voice as started to clean up my lounge. I didn't even want to think about what would have happened if I hadn't have heard anything as I picked up ceramic shards.

"Ok, we're going to have to leave your apartment tonight. It's not safe." he said, putting his phone away. "Oh, for the love of..."

I had been productive. The intruder was neatly wrapped within a cocoon of brown tape. He represented a slug in so many ways.

"I don't think you can do that-" Calloway started.

I fixed him with a furious glare. "I don't think he can break into my house, do you?"

"Touché."

We searched him and found a mobile phone. It looked pretty new, so I checked his call history. He had made received one call in the past hour and that was from an Unknown Caller.

"Well that sucks," I said, passing it to the detective.

He tucked it into his pocket and held his ribs. "Right, I'll call up some people and get this guy moved. It all right if you stay in your room for this?"

"Be my guest," I said, already walking back. If I thought it was going to be impossible to fall asleep after that, I was very very wrong.

I woke to find the mess had been cleared and a cup of coffee waiting for me. I don't usually drink coffee in the morning, but seeing that Calloway had gone to the trouble, I sneaked in a couple of sugars into it and drank it at the table.

Calloway looked exhausted. I strangely enough felt quite refreshed. Determined even. God, was I getting off on this? I opened my laptop and started checking my emails.

"Get everything sorted?"

"Yes." Calloway's shirt was creased and stained in Jack Daniel's sauce from the perp. "He's in a holding bay at the moment being questioned about what he knows."

"Won't O'Hara be suspicious?"

Calloway choked on a laugh. "He's down as being questioned for 'burglary'. O'Hara doesn't trouble himself with stuff like that."

"We'll do it today," I said, an email catching my eye. I was still avoiding Facebook. I could do without the guilt.

"Why's that?" Calloway asked, sipping his coffee.

I twisted the laptop round to him so he could read. "It's the Royal Visit today," I said, feeling my face almost break in a grin.

Calloway looked back at me, excitement wearing down the marks on his face. "PR and the Principal will be busy all morning showing them around..."

"They'll be busy all *day*, my friend." I watched him as he read the email again, making notes of times and places. I wondered how old he was. He couldn't be more than in his late twenties- thirty even at a push. His hair was dark, no greys, his skin, yeah a bit tired looking- but that was from lack of sleep.

"Ellena?"

"Um, yes?"

"You're staring at me."

"Sorry."

Ben meowed at me mockingly as I excused myself for a shower.

I never thought I would have to answer Calloway's question, for it's something I wouldn't expect to be asked by anyone.

"Why are we bringing your cat to help you break into the office?"

I muttered something under my breath and pulled on my gloves firmer.

"Ellena?"

"He's a smart cat, all right?" I snapped. "Look- I'll do the detective work and you just sit there in the getaway car, all right?"

I must have gotten to him then, because he didn't speak to me for the rest of the ride to the college. He didn't even say anything when I asked if we could stop by Boots quickly so I could pick something up.

When I got back into the car, I could tell that he was tempted to ask me what I had bought, but pride stopped him from doing so.

The College was packed- and I mean absolutely packed to the brim. Calloway's car wasn't able to stop long at the visitor's car park and he drove off unhappily to wait outside the gates of the college.

"Now you stay in there, ok?" I said into my bag.

Ben meowed a response and shuffled down grumpily, allowing me to cover him with my coat.

I peered down the hallway to Sabrina and the Principal's office whilst being swallowed by the mass of people milling about, eager to see the Duke. It was still early; 8:32am, and the Duke wasn't expected until 10am. I wondered idly if he would be punctual like expected or late like some sort of celebrity. The thought didn't last long, because I was really hungry, having skipped breakfast and I could smell bacon from the cafeteria.

I walked down the hallway quickly and dived into the toilets. I flipped the lock quickly and allowed Ben to climb out of the bag.

Now the only problem with the toilets I was in, that although the main door had a lock on it, it was actually a public set of four toilets- yes, they were a set of hardly used toilets, but if someone from Sabrina's office wanted to use them and found them locked, questions would be asked.

That was when I pulled out my purchase from Boots.

Liquid Laxative.

Now, I know what you're thinking- the office will be shut, surely? There'll be plenty of time to snoop about and find what I'm looking for. But what if they come back? What if they decide to take a break in their office, invite some of the state security to come and have a friendly chat? The Principal and PR were all about networking, and this was the corridor to do it in.

I had to make sure their day would be full of only one concern.

Their arses.

First- a diversion.

I waited for a good twenty minutes until 9am struck- that was when the tea lady came right on time, always asking the Principal first if she would like a brew.

I opened the door quickly, giving Ben his perfect opportunity. I left the toilet door slightly ajar, the screams and shrieks that followed music to my ears. Ben's meowing, hissing and spitting was the perfect backdrop to the names I was calling that pair of witches. Soon enough, Sabrina was out of the office, shrieking for security that had been specially put in place to 'dispose of that bloody ginger cat.' The office emptied to watch Sabrina spit and curse at the receptionists, whose shaking hands were apparently too slow to call pest control and security at once.

"I want that cat dealt with!" Sabrina snarled. "You hear me? Dealt with! If I have to put up with-"

I dived into the now empty office, seeing the tea tray before me. My eyes reached for the pot of tea on Sabrina's desk and with fumbling digits, I poured that sweet smelling liquid in there, the teabags promising disguise. Keys shone bright in my vision on her desk and I grabbed them. Another second passed and I was out of the office and back into the toilets, followed by a ginger ball.

My heart was pounding hard as I left the door unlocked and hid in a cubicle.

Minutes passed and I could tell by the yelling that Sabrina had returned to the office with her co-workers. I hoped briefly that the other women refused the tea, and then thought that maybe Sabrina wasn't even the person to share her brew with people.

I waited another twenty minutes, wondering what was taking so long. I looked at the bottle, but it didn't say how much time it would take. I was about to peek out of the door when it slammed open.

Heavy breathing followed as I heard the furthest away cubicle door open. Then, what I can only describe as a cry of despair was followed by something more foul smelling than Ben's litter box.

I was about to open my cubicle door when I heard the entrance open again. This time, it was another person calling for the Lord who took a cubicle next to mine. Apparently Sabrina was a sharer.

I started to make groaning noises, worried that my silence seemed suspicious, throwing in the odd grunt or too. Ben looked at me in disgust.

The door opened again and a tentative knock came on one of the doors. "Sabrina?"

"Yes, Principal?"

"...Um, the Duke will be here shortly, so I will be going to the other campus now to greet him."

"Oh God..." More unpleasant noises.

I put my hand over my mouth, partly to cover the smell, and the rest to stop myself laughing. Ben shook his head and huddled in my bag, desperate to escape the stench of rotten bowels.

"I'll be right out," groaned Sabrina.

"I'm sorry; I don't think that would be appropriate-"

"It must be food poisoning- please- I'll be right out-!"

"I'm sorry, Sabrina."

Steps came and went, and I almost felt sorry for her. Almost.

I opened the cubicle door then and went to tiptoe out when I walked into my Manager of Student Support.

I could see the horror on her face at the smell. "Oh Lord," she breathed.

"Food poisoning," I said without thinking.

The groaning ceased.

"Blackwell? Is that you?!" The realisation must have hit. "I'm going to kill you! You hear me? I'm going to kill you!"

I pulled my manager's arm and almost dragged her out of the toilets. "I'm afraid she's been like that since she's walked in," I murmured to her.

Janet's face was a picture of disbelief, shock and disgust. "Really?"

"To be honest," I said, leaning closer and starting to walk her along the hallway, "I know this sounds awful, but I'm pretty sure she's taking something."

"Like what?"

"Everything," I said. "I had a meeting with her the other day, and I kid you not, I swear she had white powder up her nose."

Janet straightened up. "She needs a doctor surely? That smell-"

"Don't worry, I'm going to stand by and make sure she's ok," I urged, ushering her away from the scene. "You've got a lot to deal with. I take it you're going over to the other campus?"

Seemingly grateful for change of subject she nodded. "Yes I am actually- oh god, the time- I must dash!"

The same time she turned, so did I, flinging open the door to Sabrina's office as I did. A huge set of brand new file cabinets were stacked against the wall and I wrinkled my nose at them, remembering my earlier breakdown with I.C.T. I walked over to them quickly and opened them. They were *huuuuge*, and hadn't really been filled with files yet. Each drawer could probably hold a large child.

There was nothing of interest in the file cabinets, so I moved to Sabrina's desk. Luckily, her computer was already on. I opened search documents and typed in *money*. About a dozen folders turned up, and I sent them to print. Whilst they were printing I searched for *accounts, Malibu, flights* and *Rino*. Nothing came up with Malibu or Rino, but I sent the rest to print.

Not happy with the documents I found, I searched in her drawers, finding a USB. Unfortunately, it required a passcode.

I typed in *Rino.*

Incorrect.

Malibu.

Nothing. I looked around for inspiration. One more attempt remaining. I carried on looking through her drawers, finding nothing but a tattered photo of an ugly mutt being hugged by a little girl, and a receipt for file cabinets. I turned the picture over.

Booglesworth 1992.

I bit my lip. Fuck it,

Booglesworth1992.

It seemed like an eternity before I saw those words- but I did.

Access granted

It was an Aladdin's Cave of deceit, lies and fake records of money. This was everything I needed and more- this was what was going to nab her and the Principal! This was what was going to free Emily!

Not sure whether the printer would keep a record of what had been printed, I put the USB into my bag. Then I saw it, next to the tea was the Official Letter from the Royal Family saying they were coming to the U.C.W to see the new Campus. Sabrina must have been bragging about it before her guts exploded. Ben jumped up to see what I was looking at.

And then Sabrina burst in.

A cat dump and a few screams later on one of the most esteemed documents the U.C.W has ever received, I was running out of there as fast as I could.

Chapter Seven

I was running around down the lane away from the college when I heard a car horn beeping me.

I slowed down to see Calloway pull up and open the door for me.

"Got it?"

"Got it!" I grinned, flashing him the USB.

"What is that?" he asked, in awe.

"Everything," I replied, stroking Ben. "But I think we've got to move to help Emily now. They won't be hanging round as soon as they realise I've taken it."

Calloway drove and didn't talk- for that I was grateful because I was too busy feeling smug with myself. I think Ben was slightly disgusted at my methods still, but hey- the plan worked.

Sabrina would be too busy emptying her bowels for the next few hours to even realise I had taken her USB.

We didn't go back to my flat, realising the possible danger. Calloway said he had two men there keeping watch inside the flat in case anyone tried to break in. I didn't know where we were going, but allowed the Detective to drive me away from Nuneaton as I rifled through the papers to see if there was anything else that could incriminate them.

I came across the file cabinet receipt and a return slip, and shrugged not knowing why I had even picked it up- yet alone why Sabrina had ordered a new set in and hadn't even filled them yet. Why had she even returned one? Surely, it was ridiculous getting something so big and expensive for an office when most files nowadays were stored in the computer.

"Another stupid expense," I said under my breath.

"What?"

"Oh, nothing- I'm just on about these massive file cabinets Sabrina ordered in. You could fit a..." My world span around for a moment.

You could fit a large child in each drawer.

"Oh my God She's returned one!" I yelled, jumping out of my seat. Calloway almost veered off the road and Ben hissed. "The cabinets! The cabinets!"

"What? What about the bloody cabinets?"

"Turn around!"

"Why?"

"Emily's in Stratford!"

"How do you know that?" Calloway demanded, pulling over, face flushed with a man who's narrowly escaped death.

"She's in the bloody cabinets that Sabrina got replaced!" See? The company that supplies them is in Stratford!"

Calloway took the receipt off me, and then I saw the dawning of realisation hit him, swiftly followed by Detective-mode. I had to admit, he was kind of sexy when he got all determined like that as we speeded down the roads towards Stratford Upon Avon. It was a weak hope. But it was still hope.

The drive was tense, and I wished he could go faster. My nails were soon destroyed by my teeth and Ben was even appearing tense. I stroked him and made soothing noises.

"What is it with you and that cat?" Calloway asked after an uncomfortable silence.

"What do you mean?"

"He goes everywhere with you."

I about to point out that dogs did the same thing with their owners, but didn't want to whilst Ben was listening. I didn't have catnip to bribe him, and I needed him on his best behaviour.

"He does what he likes, when he likes. He's goes wherever he wants whenever he wants. It just so happens that he likes to do it with me."

Calloway frowned. I hadn't given him an answer he found acceptable so he just shook his head instead.

"What is it with you and O'Hara then?" I returned.

The frown deepened. He didn't want to talk about it. "Past differences," he said vaguely. "Investigations gone wrong, evidence becoming contaminated, witnesses suddenly becoming silent." He glanced at me then. "That was when I noticed you. You didn't seem the sort to stay quiet."

"Well I'm not that," I sighed, settling back into my seat.

Stratford was a welcome sight. I actually loved it here- everything about it. Kayleigh and I used to come here when we were little and go to the Teddy Bear Museum. Whether it was still there, I didn't know, and I don't suppose Calloway was willing to take me.

We pulled up at a building on the outskirts of town. It looked respectable enough. I looked at the receipt.

"Divine Supplies," I read out. Bit cheesy, but ok. It was quieter in this area of Stratford. Not many people about. The building was detached from other buildings and looked as though it might have once been a fine character house.

"I think you should stay in the car," said Calloway peering through the window screen.

I raised my eyebrow at him. "Look- if you wanted me to stay in the car, then you shouldn't have brought me, ok?" I snapped, trying to undo my seatbelt. "I saved your damn arse when that perp broke in-"

"Perp?"

"Yeah- you heard."

"You've been watching too many detective films."

"Well, maybe you haven't been watching enough, junior." My face turning red, Ben not being helpful on my lap and my seatbelt still being jammed- I was close to screaming.

"Did you just call me Junior?"

Throwing up my hands in the air, I swallowed a howl. "Will you help me for God's sake?!"

Calloway shook his head, leant in and undid it for me. I managed to smell a whiff of mint shower gel as I did, and pretended that I didn't find the scent great.

"You need new seat belts," I muttered getting out of the car.

Divine Supplies was supposedly shut, but we could hear music coming from inside and bawdy laughter. Ben struggled out of my grasp and I set him on the floor. We walked around the back of the building, the windows blacked out, held together by flaking white wooden frames with rusted locks.

Immediately I felt suspicious that someone would black out their windows. My heart pounding hard, I tried to appear casual. Calloway opened a back gate and moved towards the back door.

Surprisingly, it was open. Ben meowed and sped past me inside. Calloway scowled at me, throwing me a look that said, "Dogs are more obedient."

The back of the office was a pit of junk. Office supplies that no one wanted, needed or hadn't even received yet. I wondered if I would recognise the cabinets that had been in Sabrina's office. Wondered if her arse had stopped exploding. Wondered if she had noticed the USB had gone. Worry started to creep in, as Calloway walked through the room and opened a door.

It probably used to be the staff room- and I say used to, because it was a mess. I realised then, that this place looked as though it had been out of business for a long time. Why order something from a business that was no longer up and running? But the thing that got me the most, was the man sitting at the table with a laptop in front of him and his trousers undone, doing what I can only describe as having the time of his life.

His eyes went from bliss to confusion to panic as he suddenly fumbled with his trousers and tried to make a run for it. Not needing to do anything but observe I watched him fall over his own laptop cable face first onto the floor.

Calloway was on him in a second. "Having a good time, were we?" he growled as he put a knee into the guy's back.

"I didn't do nothing! Ok? I didn't do *nothing!*"

Ben hissed at my side and I picked him back up. The floor was too sticky for his paws, and there were bits of glass lying about. My eyes raked over the amount of bottles, empty and half empty lying around the kitchen surfaces as Calloway demanded answers.

"Where is she?"

"I don't know nothing!"

I flinched as Calloway smacked the guy's head off the floor. "You do know where she is, tell me and we'll take it into account at your sentencing!"

To our surprise the guy started sobbing. "Ah, come on mate, my missus has just had a baby-"

"And you're mother's sick, yeah?" Calloway growled. "I've heard it all before."

"I don't know *nothing*!"

Tempted to correct his grammar, I stepped out when Calloway motioned me to. Apparently things were going to become a whole lot more unpleasant. Taking to looking around the rest of the place, I whisked Ben around in my arms, seeing if he could smell anything.

"There was a woman here," he said.

"Is it Sabrina?"

"No."

"The Principal?"

"No."

"Who?"

"Each smell doesn't come with a name tag," Ben meowed. "It would be a lot easier if you put me down."

"Ok... just be careful."

Picking his way through the debris of a business, Ben jumped up and over the office furniture, some mouldy, some broken, some still wrapped in plastic. I flinched hearing swearing in the kitchen, followed by some wailing and covered my ears.

"This smells like something," I heard Ben's muffled voice by the fireplace.

"What?" I walked over and saw a pile of thrown papers. He pawed at a pink folder. I leant down and picked it up, instantly getting a sweet scent. You didn't have to be a cat to know who the folder belonged to. I opened it up and pulled out qualifications and a C.V, all belonging to...

"Emily Baker..." I jumped up and over a chair. "She was here!" I shouted. "She was here!"

"I know," said Calloway, coming out of the kitchen wiping his hands with a kitchen towel. "And I know where she's been taken."

We left the perp taped up, Ellie-style in the kitchen. Calloway had called a couple of fellow police officers to come down and report a "burglary" for him to be taken and questioned. I was shivering with adrenaline when we got into the car.

It was starting to get dark by the time we got further into the Warwickshire Countryside. There was no saying that the address the guy had given us was real- but Calloway seemed to believe it was,

But wherever it was, Calloway wasn't sharing. My hackles started to rise up when he pulled over on a country road, another car parked with two suited people waiting outside.

"Detective Calloway, nice to see you," said a bald man, opening my door. He was dressed in a creased dark navy suit and looked as though he could do with a long sleep- or a coffee. His partner was an attractive woman in her thirties. Dark hair, dark eyes and an olive skin tone. She would have looked prettier if she smiled more, but she looked as tired as her partner.

"Miss Blackwell?" she said looking at me, in a tone that was used to soothe animals. I didn't like it. "I'm Detective Daniels. We're here to take you to a safe house."

I looked over to Calloway, aghast. "You're dumping me?"

"It's not like that," he said, not meeting my gaze. "We can't let a citizen endanger themselves." He paused then and put a warm hand on mine. "You did well, but I can't ask you to go for the next step. These are dangerous people. It may be the case that your friend-"

"Shut up," I snapped, eyes welling up. "She's alive, I know she is."

He looked up at the Detectives and nodded. "Go with them, Ellena. You can't be part of this operation."

I wanted to argue, but a sense in my said that it was utterly pointless. The two detectives outside were looking at me sympathetically, judging me as a deranged and damaged woman holding a bristling and spitting ginger cat in her lap.

"Fine," I snapped, wrestling with my seatbelt. "That's absolutely fine."

"Ellena-"

"No- I was good enough to break into her office, good enough to whack a guy over the head and save your arse, good enough to find proof that Emily was taken at the office- not to mention I was the one who found *out* she was in those cabinets in the first place-"

"Ellena- I was going to say, you just have to unclip your seatbelt."

I glared at him, and Ben hissed.

As soon as I sat in that car with the Detectives, I felt I was under arrest. Ben was put into a little cat carrier, which he hated and so did I, and placed in the open boot. I had to keep twisting around in my seat to calm him down, as I glowered at the Detective in front and the one sitting beside me.

Daniels had a handkerchief to her mouth, eyes watering. "I'm allergic," she said apologetically.

I raised my eyebrows in a 'whatever' motion and crossed my arms over my chest.

We drove to a "safe house", which was literally a B&B where they sat going over papers and talked on their phones in a private room. I didn't know what the point was in having me there or why they couldn't let me go. They believed I was in danger, they told me, and that was the end of it. I hated it- the not knowing. The room was abundant in frills, flowers and doilies. The only positive thing I could say about it was that the bathroom was nice and that it was pretty big- perfect for my pacing about.

45 minutes had passed and soon a call came from Calloway to say that the address had been hooky.

We had been screwed.

"Where did he go then?" I demanded.

"Just some flats," the bald Detective whose name I learnt was Figgs. "The man who gave that evidence is being questioned as we speak."

"So we have no leads?"

The Detectives looked uncomfortably at one another. "Not as yet."

"Would you like some coffee?" asked Daniels.

"I don't really..." An idea sprung. "Well, only if you're having some."

"I think we could all do with some coffee," laughed Figgs, trying to make light of it. "I'll call room service."

I walked over to Ben's cat carrier and stuck my fingers through, tickling him under the chin. "Marking the territory, Ben," I said.

"Meow?"

"What was that?" asked Figgs, the phone to his ear.

"Oh nothing."

The coffee service came up, including biscuits and the like, and whilst Figgs and Daniels were fussing over choosing Custard Creams and Chocolate Bourbons, I opened the cat carrier.

Havoc ensued.

Ben darted out and became a furious cloud of hissing and spitting, throwing himself about. Figgs and Daniels jumped up, almost spilling the coffee canister.

"Oh God! What's wrong with him?" I exclaimed, diving for my bag.

"How did he get out?" shrieked Daniels.

Figgs took off his jacket and tried to throw it over Ben, the clatter of car keys ringing loudly as he did. "Did you let him out?"

"Of course I didn't! It must be the cat carrier!" I rummaged through my bag quickly and pulled out the Liquid Laxative, shoving it up my sleeve. "I don't know where you got that one, but it doesn't look good quality."

I started moving towards the coffee canister.

"Oh God, my eyes are streaming- I can't see-" wailed Daniels as she ran to the bathroom.

"We only bought the damn thing this morning!" growled Figgs as he dived over the bed for Ben again.

My moment couldn't have been more perfect. I poured in the rest of the satanic liquid into the coffee canister and shoved the empty bottle in my pocket.

"Are you going to give me a hand? This is your damn cat!"

"Of course," I said, rushing to the Detective's aid. "Bennnnnnn! Bennnnn! It's all right sweetie, come to mummy." The tone in my words sickened both me and Ben, but he took it as his queue to calm down as he walked over to me, still hissing at Figgs.

I picked him up and gave him a big cuddle. "I think it's best I just keep hold of him for a while until he chills out."

"Then back in the carrier?"

"Then back in the carrier."

Figgs threw a murderous look at Ben before knocking on the bathroom door. "Daniels? It's all right- the cat's under control."

A red eyed Daniels came out, nose streaming. "I actually really like cats," she said miserably.

"You could get a sphinx?" I suggested.

Figgs continued to mutter under his breath as he poured out three cups of coffee. "Sugar, Miss Blackwell?"

It really didn't matter, because I wasn't going to drink it, but I said two anyway. I watched them carefully as they poured milk and sugar into their own coffees-Daniels, unashamedly putting three heaped spoons in.

"Here's your coffee," Figgs said, offering it to me.

"Oh, can you put it on the side, please? I'll have it in a minute. Hands full, you see."

He nodded and took a big slurp out of his own drink. He frowned, looking at it strangely.

My heart stopped.

"Need more sugar," he mumbled. "My wife keeps telling me to cut down, but one sugar in coffee just doesn't do anything."

I held back a sigh of relief as I watched him dump in another sugar, and then cheekily a half more. Daniels was grinning at him.

"So, Miss Blackwell," she said, turning to me with her own cup between her hands. "Have you been at the U.C.W long?"

I launched into a conversation about the college, not because I wanted to, but to keep them drinking their coffee. They drank it pretty quickly and helped themselves to another cup- I must have been boring them.

"Your drink's going to get cold," Daniels commented.

"Oh, it doesn't matter," I said, leaning over to the tray. "I think I'll just have a biscuit."

The female Detective shied away from Ben hanging in my arms as I picked up a couple of custard creams. It was only then when I realised how hungry I was. I crushed up a biscuit and offered it to Ben, who clearly wasn't interested.

They downed that cup of coffee and had a third. My eyes were watering at the sight of these detectives glugging down that black liquid, busy calling colleagues, and checking out evidence.

"Do you have the recording?" Daniels asked me, finishing her third cup.

"Yeah," I said, pulling out my new phone. It wasn't as posh as my other one, but I had managed to download some files from my computer onto it, including some nice chubby photos of Rowan, which I showed to her much to her delight. Figgs wasn't as impressed.

"I've had five kids, Miss Blackwell," he said. "Once you've seen one baby, you've seen all of them."

Daniels disagreed with him, which made me feel even guiltier of what was to come swiftly their way. I opened the recording file and played it to them, the odd stomach rumble from them being the only thing that interrupted it.

"Ooh, sorry," Daniels apologised, putting a hand on her stomach. "It must have been that Subway."

The recording played on.

"Apparently his new bitch loves horses. I'd rather pull down my inheritance brick by brick, tree by tree than have her house her stupid ponies in there."

I frowned then. Something was nagging at the back of my mind. Suddenly, Daniels looked a bit uncomfortable and then jumped up. "Excuse me," she said, face red and rushed to the toilet, the hard lock loud as it snapped into place.

Groans very similar to Sabrina's followed. Figgs stood up and asked tentatively if she was ok.

I shook my head and tapped the screen to go back in the recording.

"Right. Have you sorted out the accounts?"

"All done."

"Good. This divorce is going to cost me. I'm not letting him have the farmhouse in Stratford."

"Why would he want that?"

I jumped up at the same time as Figgs started banging at the toilet door, clutching his stomach. "Let me in, Daniels!"

"Oh God...! What was in... that Subway Sandwich?"

"Daniels, for the love of God, let me in this room!"

"Are you ok, Detective Figgs?" I asked, mock shock on my face.

"No!" he yelled unashamedly. "My arse is about to cave in!"

"I think I saw some public toilets downstairs?" I offered.

The look of hope lit up his face for half a second before his stomach growled, bending him in half. He turned to me then, and pointed a shaking finger at me. "You.Stay.*Here.*"

I nodded dumbly as he ran out of the room. I waited for two seconds before I grabbed his jacket and dug out his keys from the pocket.

Good. This divorce is going to cost me. I'm not letting him have the farmhouse in Stratford.

The Principal's words echoed in my head, over and over again.

This divorce is going to cost me. I'm not letting him have the farmhouse in Stratford.

I opened the door to the room, my bag already slung over my shoulder and Ben at my feet. "Let's go, Ben!"

I'm not letting him have the farmhouse in Stratford.

Farmhouse in Stratford.

Farmhouse in Stratford.

Farmhouse in Stratford.

I stopped my run as soon as I got to reception, quickly only when I heard moaning come from the public toilets and stepped out into the cold air of freedom.

I walked to the black rover the detectives had driven me here by and unlocked it without a moment's hesitation.

I had 30 minutes tops before the detectives managed to scramble their way back into the world of the living and find me gone. Thankfully, I had seen both of their phones on the coffee table in the room, so there was no chance of them making any calls whilst they were cemented to porcelain.

I had never driven any other car except from my KA, and my driving instructor's.

"No worries," I said, putting the keys in the ignition.

"I wish there were seat belts for cats," Ben meowed.

I drove not really knowing where I was going to be honest. The radio in the car buzzed a couple of times, but I was too confused, and admittedly a bit scared to answer it. I was breaking the law. I was stealing a car.

If Sabrina and the Principal weren't going to prison after this, then I certainly was.

"Ok, so we're looking for a farmhouse on a patch of land in Stratford..." I murmured, pulling up on the side of the road.

Thankfully, someone genius had invented Google, and some divine being had decided that my signal was going to work that day.

I typed *Principal University College of Warwickshire* into Google, found her husband, Karl Bowers, and some pictures of them together.

Some were towards a charity do, some were at a political conference, others were with the Mayor, but one photo was all I needed.

A couple, arms around each other holding a glass of champagne each posed in front of the camera in front of a derelict farm house.

I clicked on it and found the news page to go with it.

It was a news article from 2002 talking about the renovation plans to do up a piece of Stratford's history, an old Saxon building that had been used over time, until it had been used as a cattle holding in the 18th century. I skipped the history lesson and found the name of the farm.

Aldrith Farm.

I drove on until I found some country walkers. "Excuse me," I said, putting down the window. "Can you tell me where Aldrith Farm is, please?"

The two country walkers, who I took were married came over with two collies and looked curiously to Ben sitting in the passenger seat.

"You have a cat in your car," the old man remarked, looking dumbfounded.

I shrugged casually. "Your dogs like to walk- he prefers to be driven, what can I say?"

The walker frowned at me as if I had gone mad.

"Aldrith farm is that way five miles out," his wife said helpfully, cheeks red from the cold wind. "Follow the signs for Pennington and it's there."

"Wonderful- thank you!"

The roads got narrower as I followed her instructions. I think I got lost a couple of times and then I saw that glorious sign.

Aldrith Farm.

I pulled up in front of it, my heart beating. I pulled out my phone and considered calling Calloway. I looked at Ben as if for answers but he was involved in a much more important task of grooming himself.

I swore and pressed DIAL.

Calloway picked up on the second ring.

"Calloway here?"

I flinched at his formal greeting. "Err, hi, it's Ellena-"

"Ellena! Where are you?"

Remembering that I hadn't given him my new number, (which in hindsight is probably a stupid thing to forget) I ploughed on. "Look- you can shout at me later, but I'm outside the Principal's place in Stratford- it's a place called Aldrith Farm-"

"Why? Why are you there? You wait there for me, you hear?"

"No- I've got to check this out-"

"Listen Ellena, this is not a game," Calloway growled. "You are not a cat with nine lives, ok?"

I looked down at Ben, rubbing his head against my arm, purring contentedly. He would go anywhere with me. I smiled and rubbed his ears, ignoring Calloway. Sometimes you just have to decide what is right and wrong in life. You can stand here and allow things to happen, or you can do something about it.

Besides, things never worked out when I waited for people to make it happen with me.

"I'm going in, Arthur," I said.

He started to splutter on the other end, I know, trying to find the right words that would make me stop.

"What's wrong, Detective?" I said finally. "Cat got your tongue?"

"Ellena!"

I hung up.

The hill was a downward slope. It was muddy, cold and frozen in patches. I almost slipped a couple of times and I was thankful that Ben had his winter coat on. I could see the dilapidated farmhouse below past a cluster of trees. There were car tracks across the field, so someone had been here recently.

I pulled my coat tighter around myself. I had hidden the car down another lane and walked the rest of the way.

"Ben, if we're both going to die today, don't you want to tell me how you came back?"

"We're not going to die today, silly human."

"But don't you want to tell me?"

He walked on ahead of me, tail high, fur burning brightly in the frost. "You don't need to know how everything happens, Ellena."

"How can you talk?"

He was silent.

"You're never going to tell me, are you?"

"I don't need to," he said. "You'll find that out for yourself one day."

We were quiet then for a while as we ploughed on. "I tried to change your name to Aslan when I was little," I said, suddenly remembering.

"You did."

"It never stuck."

"It didn't." He rubbed against me. "Like I said- my name is Benedict."

I rolled my eyes and began to feel the true effects of fear as the farmhouse came close. It was strange. It was as if I was walking in a dream, as though my body was not my own. I didn't want to think too much of it in case I ran away. It looked as though some renovation had been attempted on it in the past, but it had been given up on halfway through. It could be quite a pretty building, I thought. One story and long, its bright walls were made of sandstone. Someone had strapped tarpaulin over the windows and put metal sheeting where there wasn't glass. The wind whistled through it sharply, and I dug my hands further into my pockets.

I hunkered down at the side of the wall and pulled Ben closer.

"Can you skirt around and see if there's anyone inside? Check out the situation?"

He licked my hand. "Of course."

"I'll wait here."

I watched as he slinked off into the cold. A fog had started to rise and it sent my senses screaming. My boots were sinking in the mud and my leggings were damp already from the drizzle that had started to fall. My nose twitched, the smell of moss and mould surrounding me.

I held my breath, hoping Ben was all right. Seconds may have passed but it felt like an age. A rustling came behind me and I breathed a sigh of relief as I turned round.

"Anything, Ben?" I asked, just in time to see the blow that knocked me out.

Chapter Eight

I don't know how long I was out for, but when I blearily opened my eyes I realised my face was half engulfed in mud. Making little movement, I turned my head.

Shapes danced ahead, until I realised they weren't shapes but people. Warmth trickled onto my nose from my forehead and down my cheek. I wasn't a genius, but even I knew it was blood. God, I felt sick.

"What do we do with her now?" growled a voice.

I shut my eyes again, pretending to be unconscious, all the while my brain dancing about, grabbing information as I could.

"We've got to split. The money is being transferred tomorrow morning. Flights leave tonight."

"What do we do with these two then?"

"Put them with the others."

Others?

I wondered where Ben was, but when I tried to move my hands and feet, I realised that they were tied. Strange that the first fear that came into my mind was for my cat and not me. I could have laughed.

I stiffened when I saw boots approach me through slitted eyes, could taste the dust and mud he unsettled as he came closer. Hands roughly scooped me up and lifted me. Unwilling to go anywhere this guy was taking me, I kicked out and was promptly dropped.

The man swore and kicked me, earning a yelp that I only realised minutes later was mine.

"She said the name 'Ben'," he growled. "There's a dude sniffing around here, I know it."

"We'll keep an eye out for him then, won't we?"

I flinched, my hazy memory trying to recollect the voice it belonged to.

"No witnesses! That's what you said!"

"Exactly. Now come on- we've got some gasoline to pick up." This voice, I realised suddenly was Rino's.

"Yeah," the man said. "This place is going to go up like a torch, little girl. BOOM!" He laughed then and kicked me once more for good measure.

I groaned and curled up into a little ball.

I realised, a while later that I had passed out again and had woken up for the second time. It was pitch black, and something warm was licking my face.

"Ben?" I muttered.

"Yes, silly human," he meowed softly. "Those rats have gone, but there is another one outside keeping watch."

I moaned again. Blood was salty in my mouth and I wondered when I had bitten my tongue.

"Can you sit up?" he asked.

I tried, but my legs were wrapped really tight. It took a couple of attempts before I managed it, and even then I almost passed out again.

"I wish I was a lion," Ben said woefully.

"I don't. I love you just the way you are."

This earned some mores licks from Ben. I shuffled backwards so the wall was supporting my back and took a breather.

"There's another person here," Ben said, settling into my lap.

I took a deep breath and started to wriggle to the place Ben said they were. A curled up ball of limbs was huddled in the corner of the darkness that was supposedly a room.

"Hello?" I whispered. "Oh god, Ben, I need my hands. Can you chew through the duct tape?"

Ben set to it, biting my skin more than a few times. I held back my grunts of pain, trying to concentrate making out the shape of the unconscious person. I pulled my wrists as hard as I could, trying to stretch out the tape and then would let Ben carry on chewing. It was an agonisingly slow procedure.

"Hurry up!" I hissed.

"This...doesn't...taste....very nice...you know..." he growled between bites.

Suddenly, lights from the car illuminated the place; shards of yellow seeping through the cracks were the metal sheets couldn't cover, exposing unmistakable long blonde hair of the person next to me.

"Emily!"

She didn't move, or turn her face to me. Nothing.

"Ben! Hide!"

But he was already gone. Clever cat.

The doors opened and Rino and his buddy walked in carrying barrels of oil. Oh this was not looking good.

They were both swaying slightly and I took it for granted that they had been drinking.

"Oh, she's moved has she? Gone to see your little friend, have you?"

"Keith, shut the fuck up, will you?"

I would love to tell him exactly what I thought of him there and then, but I wasn't stupid. The men ignored me then as they carried on drinking, checking their watches and laughing at a stupid joke. I pulled on my wrists as hard as I could and jumped when it actually snapped.

Damn. The cat was good.

"All right, what are we waiting for then?" Keith said. "I'll do a couple of lines first then set to it."

My hands shuffled behind me, looking for something- searching for a lifeline in the dark. Cold mud shoved its way under my fingernails, glass shards nipping my skin and slicing my knuckles. My muscles ached and it hurt to breathe, making me wonder if I had cracked any ribs. It made no sense to think of it now.

My desperate eyes fell onto Emily and I wondered just how injured she was. I didn't want to think what they had done to her, but the inevitable thoughts pushed their way into my head and made my movements more frantic. Nudging her with my knee, I was rewarded with a groan. "*Emily!*" I whispered. "We've got to get out of here!"

Another groan. I wanted to reach out with my hands to check her over but didn't dare move in case Rino found my hands free.

Footsteps crunched the stray pebbles on the ground. "You messed with the wrong people," Rino said finally coming into view, white powder shining from his nose. He looked as though he had slept in the black suit he was wearing, his burgundy striped shirt stained, his hair a mess and his face unshaven. I wondered what he had been through since I saw him last and then decided I didn't care.

That was when I saw it.

A canister of oil was in his hands.

I looked from the canister to his face and then back again. Whatever expression I had on my face must have amused him because a huge grin suddenly broke on his face.

"I suppose you're wondering what this is?" he purred, waving it about, the sloshing sound of its contents loud in my ears.

I kept my retort bitten down and watched as he walked lazily around the debris of crates, hay and old farming equipment, his hand starting to twist around the cap.

"No? Oh smart girl has worked it out." He winked at me and started to drip it around the dilapidated barn. "I warned you, didn't I, sweetheart?"

Silence was his only reward for goading me, but I'm sure he liked the sound of his own voice.

Keith was smiling behind Rino as he lined up his powder on a sheet of metal. He made grunting noises as he slid his face over it, coughing at one point and then starting again. I hoped he breathed in a shard of glass.

Rino had started to hum under his breath as he pranced around the room in a seemingly drunken dance, as if he was watering flowers and not preparing to send me up in flames.

It's strange when you feel your time run out. An inevitable moment of clarity where you know it's either flight or fight. You have a choice of doing something-being proactive. I thought of my nephew, that beautiful baby and what he would think when he grew up when he found his auntie couldn't fight back- didn't fight back. I felt a sudden huge regret that clenched my stomach so hard it made me unable to breathe.

"Hey Keith- go and get the others why don't you?" Rino snapped as Keith rubbed his face clear from the last line. "Let's finish this. I've got a flight to catch."

"Going somewhere nice?" I asked, unable to help myself, my fingers stretching out behind me in a spiderlike dance, still searching, grasping.

Rino stopped pouring gasoline for a moment and actually smiled. "Something like that," he said.

I smiled back, blood filming my teeth in a salty manic grin, something colder than the earth meeting my insect hands finally. Something hard and unforgiving.

My smile disturbed him, I could tell because he started to step towards me. "I don't know why you're grinning like a Cheshire Cat," Rino spat, then changing direction to Emily. Then, his eyes narrowing into a smile more manic than my own, lifted the canister can.

My nostrils flared in panic as I watched the liquid splash down on Emily, soaking her clothes and filling the air with that strong chemical stench. Still, she didn't move, a bare whisper of a whimper coming from her core.

I took a breath. He was goading me.

"I do," I said, and that was when I hit him. My arm snaked out in one long arc as I hit him full force in the stomach, a metal cattle prod revealing itself in the sickly yellow light as my weapon.

He fell, winded and rolled on the floor, just as Keith waddled in. "Hey, Rino, do you want them brought in separately or-" His fat form swayed at the sight of the boss grunting in pain. "What the-"

Just then, a ginger ball of claws and teeth lunged onto his face. Keith screamed, wrestling with a furry demon of fury. "Rino! Help me!"

I scrambled with my feet, pulling off my boots and the tape with them (haven't they watched detective films? always tape the ankles!)

"I'm gonna get you, you little bitch!" snarled Rino, grabbing my foot.

My breath caught as I kicked him in the face, grabbing Emily from under the shoulders. She whimpered as I dragged her across the floor, the world spinning from my head injury. I halted, realising Rino had opened up his lighter.

"Stop right there, missy," he said, blood leaking from a cut eyebrow. "One more step and your mate is roasted and toasted."

My eyes widened at Emily's gasoline soaked trousers. I swallowed.

"Now that's it. Sit down like a good girl."

My heart pounding, Keith's screams suddenly quiet outside, I realised that maybe this really was it.

I sat down, grasping Emily's freezing hand. "You don't need her anymore," I growled. "You can just go on your sunny holidays and leave her!"

He tutted, shaking his dark head. "Ah now, you see, I can't do that. People have to die here tonight." He pulled out something from his back pocket I had never seen before.

A gun.

"Now, don't worry, this isn't my gun- this is the Principal's husband's gun, but I suppose that don't matter does it?"

"Not to me," I muttered.

"Well, you see it should." He knelt then in front of me and held my bloody chin tightly in his rough fingers. I realised then that I had cut his lip, the red oozing in a bloody lump. "You see, you made my girlfriend shit herself, it only seems right that I should do the same to you. That's why I'm gonna tell you. I want you to know everything that's gonna happen to you."

It seemed a weird logic, but I was beyond caring. I wondered if Ben was ok. Was he hurt? I hoped he would run away. Find a nice new owner.

"Enlighten me," I grunted.

"You see, the people we have in the boot is the Principal's ex and his new missus." His smile widened at my look of horror. "That's right- the Principal's ex is a sicko. He likes to snatch employees of the U.C.W. He took your friend, then you and shot you both. His girlfriend walked in, and in surprise he shot her too. Then, too ashamed and horrified at his actions, he then sets the place on fire and shoots his brains out."

"You're mental," I said finally.

His self-pleased smile fell. "Yeah? And what have you ever achieved? You're lying here in the muck about to have your brains blown out." He hit me then. "Then I'm gonna torch your body. Watch you burn. No one's gonna be able to tell it's you by the time they hose this place down and drag your corpses out!"

He leaned closer, his stubble poking out from olive skin, dark eyes gleaming, and a new idea playing on his mind as he looked me up and down. I have only had glimpses of evil before. I used to work at a prison

and you could see small flashes in it in people's stories-
see it in the news from the result of their actions. But I
had never seen it this clear before. This delight of chaos.
This pleasure in inflicting pain. This sadistic and
twisted calculated manoeuvre of cruelty.

Like a wild cat, I threw myself at him, knocking
the lighter from his hand and away from Emily. He
grunted in surprise as I hit him as hard as I could in the
face. The gun went off, and suddenly shouting was all
around me. Dazed by sudden light flooding into the
room, I punched Rino again before falling off, feeling
hands at my throat.

He was winning, his fingerprints pressing down in
the tender flesh around my jugular. His bloody lips
curled back in a dog-like snarl, I could do all but stare
hatefully back at evil as I clawed at his hands, my head
crunching lower and lower into the mud.

I blinked, sirens booming in my ears as the air
struggled to reach my lungs. Suddenly, I could breathe,

hands away from my throat, the weight gone from my body. I heaved precious oxygen into my body before rolling onto my front, my eyes locking with Emily's filthy face. Her eyes were open.

I think I actually laughed in relief.

Sitting up, I crawled over to her as police flooded the cattle barn, Rino's shouts ringing off the walls.

She blinked at me, whatever patch of skin that wasn't covered in bruises or dried blood was smudged in dirt. Her fingers twitched as though she was trying to reach for my hand. I grabbed it.

"Ellie," she whispered. "...You've got red all on you."

"Ellena, you here?"

Calloway's voice almost dragged me out of the confusion, as I looked from Emily down to my stained shirt. I reached to touch the spreading dampness from my middle and turned to see the Detective suck in a breath. My apologetic smile cracked my face.

"Nine lives, ay?"

"Ellena!"

I don't know what it was, but I was suddenly unable to keep my balance. I fell away from Emily, her fingers slipping from mine as the freezing floor became a bed for my aching body.

Calloway's white face floated above mine.

"I need an emergency unit here now!" he shouted, his hands on my stomach.

"Ben- find Ben-"

"Shut up, Ellena, just breathe." He turned to shout more instructions at a colleague on a radio.

"Don't... worry," I said, my tongue feeling useless and numb. "It doesn't...hurt."

"Don't worry," he said. "Everything's going to be..."

His voice dazed off, and all I could hear was that long mournful meow.

My Granddad was sitting in his favourite chair again, waiting for me, with an Alsatian asleep at his feet. I smiled, glad to finally be warm, surrounded by the safest place I knew. His house.

"Is this Shezzi?" I asked, giving the sleepy dog a tickle behind the ears.

"It is."

"You found her then?"

"I think she found me!" my Granddad laughed.

"Where's Ben?" I asked.

"He's looking for you," Granddad said. "'Ere' come give us a cuddle."

I smiled and went over to him. His stubble rubbed my cheek, the scent of oil, tea, David Beckham (Granddad's favourite aftershave, though I doubted he knew who he was) filled my senses. It was such a comforting smell and I didn't want to let go.

His hand was huge in mine, and I found myself holding it to it tightly, letting his warmth flow into my skin.

"You asked me, Ellena, and I'm here."

"Asked you what, Granddad?"

"To get you when it's your turn."

I would have felt panic, but it was hard to in this place. "Is it my turn?"

"That depends."

"Is Ben still looking for me?"

Granddad nodded.

I sighed then, happy and content. "I love you, Granddad."

He smiled at me, his hair neatly combed and newly cut. Pulling me into his thick armed embrace he squeezed me. "I love you too," he said. "You are such a good granddaughter."

Scratching was coming from the front door, incessant meows interrupting the moment.

"Don't leave me, Granddad," I started to cry.

He laughed softly and gave me another squeeze. "You silly girl," he said. "Now why would I ever do that?"

The meowing was getting louder.

"Granddad?"

"He's here to take you back."

"Granddad!"

"Come on, Shez. Time to go." Granddad was smiling as he gave me a kiss on my cheek, Shezzi standing to attention at his side. And as I watched him stand up from his chair, I noticed that there had been no winces, aches or pains. He needed no help at all.

I realised in the days after that, that I was in hospital. I was unable to talk, weak and on a lot of pain relief. I had never been on morphine before, but it was lovely.

Sometimes I imagined Ben lying on the bed with me, purring away, but I knew that couldn't be the case. Calloway had told me in one of my conscious moments that they had been unable to find him. In one of my insane moments (which were more frequent) I had ranted and raved to my family to drive to Stratford to try and find him. Police were still in the area gathering evidence and had promised to pick him up if they found him.

But what if he was hurt? It was freezing outside, no houses around for miles!

I sank into a despairing pit that no one seemed able to drag me out of, and allowed sleep to be my new reality.

It was my sister that pulled me out of it.

She had brought Rowan in one day. That big bundle of scowls, pouted lips and various high pitched noises became my new lifeline.

"It was Ben, you know," I said.

Kayleigh smiled sadly at me, eyeing my new morphine drip. Rowan sleeping in her arms, content in his Led Zeppelin baby grow I had bought him. I think she had put it on him to cheer me up.

"It was him Kayleigh. From Tamworth." I started to cry. "It was him."

"Go to sleep, Ellena."

So I did.

I wished I could sleep forever. In my dreams Ben was there, lying next to me, purring softly. I could feel his fur against my skin as I slept. Sometimes when I awoke, I would find Calloway there. Face pale, shadows under his eyes and stubble getting longer.

"You need to shave," I said groggily. Someone had told me the day before that I had gotten pneumonia as well as the broken ribs, concussion and a gunshot wound.

Lucky me.

"You need to get better," he said seriously. His tie was in his hand, his shirt and grey suit rumpled.

"Emily?"

"She's recovering with her family," he said.

I nodded. "The perps?"

A sad smile broke his face, lightening it up for a moment. I liked it. "We got them, Ellena."

"We did?"

"Yeah. Thanks to you." He shifted then. "Although I don't think Figgs and Daniels will be thankful to you."

I laughed. "Stop it," I wheezed. "It hurts!"

"Sorry."

The paper soon wanted to interview me, and then surprisingly, the Manager of Foundation Learning did too. He spoke to me briefly, my mum tapping her shoe impatiently behind him.

"If you think she's going back to work in that place, you've got another thing coming," she snarled, arms crossed over her chest.

Jeff shifted uncomfortably. "We heard about Ben," he said, "we are all really sorry-"

"He's not gone," I said icily, the morphine bringing a manic edge to my voice. "He's not gone, he's just lost!" The tears started to fall then again. God I was tired of crying.

"We, err, got you a card..." Jeff said, passing it me.

Mum helped me open it, and I saw it was actually a picture of Ben and me walking to work. One of the students had taken it and put it up on Facebook apparently. It was signed by all of the staff in student support, my fellow English Teachers, as well as my Learners. It made me wail all the more.

Jeff handed my mother another package then, quickly made his excuses and left. Mum held me as the nurse gave me something to calm me down.

I was very ill the next few days and I can't remember much. If there was anything to catch at the hospital- I got it. I remembered my Granddad's time at the hospital and suddenly wished I had asked him to take me with him.

But Ben had found me.

And I couldn't find him now.

The scandal was still playing out when I finally got out of hospital. I had lost more weight and couldn't go back to work for a while. Nuneaton Academy had sent me a letter, wishing for me to get better, saying they were looking forward to me delivering the Creative Writing Course, and University College of Warwickshire had assured me my job was still waiting for me when I got back.

Emily and I met up a couple of times. We didn't have to say much. We just hugged and watched films together, mostly Disney.

"I think I'm going to go away travelling," she said suddenly one day.

"Yeah?" I asked, seeing that the shadows under her eyes were as dark as my own.

"My sister wants to take me. I think I'm going to do it. Get away from here a while."

I nodded numbly. "You should."

That was all we said on the matter.

As for the Principal and Sabrina, they had been apprehended at the airport, one at the bar and one clutching a toilet. I'll leave you to decide who was doing what.

Rino and his chums were also being sentenced, as well for a bunch of other crimes. I hoped they got life. The Principal's ex, Kirk Bowers and his fiancée Emma Cook were slowly getting back to their lives, but were first going to enjoy a long holiday in the Caribbean. He had successfully divorced his ex-wife and had donated the Aldrith Farm to a Donkey Sanctuary. He said that he had always seen his ex-wife as an ass, so it seemed fitting.

Jake O Hara was due to sentencing for his part in the case and for several others that had been brought to light. Calloway had a stack of files ready to be reviewed against O'Hara. He wasn't going to miss a chance like this to let Jake walk away.

I stayed at home for a while before returning to my flat, much to my mother's horror. Andy had come back from Australia in the wake of the drama and had spent some time with me.

"You need to get your life back," he said sitting with me in Costa.

I stared down into my hot chocolate, not caring.

"Get some flesh on your bones."

I shifted, uncomfortably. "I'm drinking the fattiest thing here, aren't I?"

He frowned at me. "Why don't you come back with me and your mum to Australia? Just for a few months? Could be good for you."

I thought of Emily, remembering the look in her eyes when she spoke about leaving. She had gotten on a plane last week, had invited me to her going away party. I had gone, but hadn't stayed for long. Every shout, laugh and clink of glasses made me jump. People had become uneasy around me unsure of what to say to the damaged goods.

"I'll think about it," I finally said.

My dad left it at that and started talking about Rowan.

Mum had sat down with me and opened the letter Jeff had given me. It was a proposal of starting a Creative Writing Course at the U.C.W. They hadn't done A-Levels there for 2 years, but reading my emails and thinking it over, they had decided to give it a go- as long as I agreed to be Leader of the Course. It was to start in the Summer. My hands fingered the corners of the paper, breath catching. It was April now, the snow had gone and still no news of Ben.

Detective Figgs and Detective Daniels came to visit me with Calloway to brief me on what had happened. Calloway had sent a team to the farm as soon as he had gotten off the phone to me, and Figgs and Daniels took the rest of the week off work, having some rather severe food poisoning. I wasn't sure whether Calloway had told them about the liquid laxative, so I kept quiet, planning to choose another moment to admit it if it ever cropped up again.

I wasn't to get into any trouble about stealing the car in hindsight of what was at risk. They all agreed that if I hadn't had done what I had done then Rino and Rick could have set the place alight with everyone in it, making a hasty getaway. We would have lost them.

Calloway had been liaising with the college for me, as I hadn't the heart to talk to them about what had happened. He passed me an official letter of thanks from the New Acting Principal.

My mother had collected the news stories about the incident, although she never told me. The pile of papers in the shoe cupboard was evident, and not a very good hiding place.

I never regretted what had happened. I made a choice. I had done the right thing. But it had come at a cost. I had to rebuild my life, but I was finding every day more exhausting than the one previous. It was as if the entire situation had revealed so many people's true colours. People called the house wanted a news story, friends came to the house wanting to know the gossip-not really concerned with me, but more because they wanted to be seen as the person who knew the chick who got shot.

I had become a novelty.

My real friends were the ones that allowed me to forget it for a while. Came over to try and give me normalcy, and when they saw that that sometimes was just too much, gave me space. I just wanted my family around me.

I became edgy, flinching at the door knocking or the bell ringing. I was suspicious of every car, convinced that Rino still had friends out there.

Calloway assured me that they had been taken care of and said that they had the place under surveillance. I wasn't sure whether he was lying just to make me feel better, but it was a comfort in any case.

Chapter Nine

The day soon came to relive it all over again. I was sick telling people the same thing over and over again. The story had been all over the news now and I had even had a gossip magazine ask for an interview. Calloway was a calming presence, and talked me through it.

I had to give evidence.

I hated listening to when they questioned Calloway, but his strength gave me some hope. He threw me a wink as he went up.

"Can you please tell the jury what you saw when you first entered the barn," The Prosecution said, her voice loud and booming off the Warwick Court walls.

Calloway straightened and folded his hands before him, and I could see there in his eyes the same horror that I had seen when he found me.

"I saw Mr Gavinchi being pulled from Miss Blackwell," he said.

"And then?"

His jaw tightened. "Then she turned around when I called her name." He paused, his expression unreadable. "She was covered in blood, but more so in the stomach area. I realised that she had been shot."

"And what did you do then?"

"We secured Mr Gavinchi and called the emergency services," Calloway answered.

Images of that moment filled my eyes. His face floating above mine. His skin whitening as he put pressure on my stomach. Shouting. Sirens. Radio signals. Swearing. Pleading.

Cat lives... I thought. *I'm running out of cat lives.*

Then it was my turn to give evidence. I used the last of my mental strength by blocking out the Principal's lawyer from my mind. It was endless, full of questions about my conduct, how I had managed to find the USB, why I went through the computer, why did I go to Stratford. The defending Lawyer even suggested at one point that there was an ulterior motive in it for me.

Luckily, the jury knew bullshit when they smelt it. A news campaign later, a weekly drive down to Stratford, and several drunken binges later, the people who had nearly ruined my life were sentenced. I didn't ask for how many years, just, "Is it a long time?" when Calloway came knocking on my door.

He nodded grimly.

"Do you want to come in?"

He cleared his throat and made a small nod, so I took that as a yes. I walked to the kitchen and started to boil the kettle.

"Tea or coffee?" I asked.

"Anything without liquid laxative."

I laughed then, the sound strange to my own ears.

He came over quite a lot then, just to check up on me, he said.

I didn't mind. It gave me a reason to shower and put a dab of makeup on. I realised after a while that my hair was getting on and my roots were showing. My mum was pleased when I had Skype called her to let her know I was going to the hairdressers. She had gone back to Australia with my dad after I had told them I wouldn't be coming over- not yet anyway.

"It's about time you started looking after yourself, Ellena," she said tentatively. "Maybe it's time to let Ben go."

My breath caught and I mumbled something about missing my appointment before shutting off the call.

The women at the hairdressers cooed at me and trying egging me into conversation, but I couldn't contribute. I told them I was suffering from a bug so couldn't talk. I had my hair re highlighted and my roots touched up. I could tell they wanted me to talk to them about what had happened. My face had been splashed around the news enough for strangers to know my name.

I thanked them when I left, not sure if I should have gone for a complete change of style instead. Maybe people would stop recognising me then.

Sometimes in my bad moments, I thought I saw the flash of ginger when I was walking about. I had nearly stolen a neighbour's ginger cat, thinking it was Ben. The old lady had chased me down the street, shouting at me, before they realised who I was.

"Not that one, dear," the old woman said cautiously, pulling the wriggling fur ball from my arms. "This is Milly." Milly is *my* cat."

"I'm looking for Ben," I said numbly.

"Well maybe he's looking for you too," she said and walked away before I could apologise.

More days passed and my auntie came to visit me.

She sat me down on the sofa, my Nan and my brother in law in the kitchen, cooing over Rowan. Kayleigh was taking a rare afternoon off to have her nails seen to, and Sharon had come down especially to see me.

"How are you honey?" she asked. My auntie was the perfect person to open up to. I don't know why, but whenever I saw her, everything poured out in a wave.

I stared at her, her blonde hair pulled back into a ponytail. I used to think she and my mother were sisters when I was little. I think my mother liked that. My mother was one daughter with four brothers, and I didn't have to guess twice to think that she may have wished for a sister.

"Ok," I said. I paused, looking back up at her. I bit my lip. "I've lost him."

"Who have you lost, honey?" she said, leaning over and taking my hand.

"Everything?" How could I describe the meaning of a cat to someone? How could I explain that I had lost the only person who truly knew what I was like? He had been sent here for a reason- and I had lost him. He had helped me so much, and I had left him in that freezing cold in Stratford. I had failed him again. He had filled the crater my Granddad had left behind. Who would guide me now?

"Granddad came to me," I said then.

Sharon blinked in surprise. "Did he?"

"He asked if I wanted to go with him," I said, swallowing more tears. "And I stayed. I stayed."

Sharon took me back to the doctors, my mother waiting in Sharon's office as I spoke to the expert. He diagnosed me with depression, and I suddenly felt it had all been for nothing.

I was back at stage one.

My family were worried about me, and it was making me anxious. It burnt at my back, making me jump with their phone calls, their knocking, their tip toeing around. They wanted me to get better faster.

They didn't like what I had become, and I didn't either. My mother said she wanted to understand. She wanted me to tell her everything. I allowed Calloway to take her call and explain everything. I couldn't do it. She could read what happened in the newspapers if she liked.

"I'll tell you one day, mum," I promised.

Except about the talking cat.

I didn't want to go to the nutty farm. I started to pretend I was getting better. Writing false emails to my parents that I was ok. I dodged calls from Calloway, pretending I wasn't in when he knocked. My hair grew longer, my nail varnish chipped, my roots darkened again and the food was always out of date in my fridge.

Emily sent me postcards, which was nice. They were the only colourful thing in my kitchen, held up by magnets on the fridge. She was having a great time with her sister, and had even made some friends. Her sister was coming back this month, but she was going to carry onto Thailand with the people she had met.

I was happy for her, and braved Facebook one day to send her a message. I had about a hundred notifications and hundreds of messages, but I ignored them all. A moment of insanity came to me and I clicked on Ben's Facebook Page.

It was my undoing.

A bottle of rum later, I passed out of the floor, seeing ginger flashes everywhere.

Sometimes I drank just to fall asleep. It was too difficult without. I would lie awake else, my eyes staring at the ceiling, playing over the same scenes over and over again. My Granddad was sitting in his chair again. No Shezzi and no Ben.

"Nan misses you," I told him.

He smiled. "Well what is she doing? I'm around!"

"She says she can't see you."

He winked at me then, dropping crumbs from a biscuit onto his cardigan. "She's not looking in the right places, Ellena. And neither are you."

Not looking in the right places?

I stared at his cardigan, knowing that it was currently in my wardrobe in my room. I had only owned it for two months before I lost a button. I still felt guilty about it.

"You're not looking in the right places, Ellena."

Right place.

A taxi drove me to St Wildred's at 8:43 in the morning. I was still drunk and the taxi driver was too polite to say anything. I wasn't too drunk however to wait for my five pound change.

The bells were ringing for service- the only inclination I had that it was Sunday. I winced at the sound and trudged my way to the other side of the church yard, minding the bluebells as I went.

How many times had I taken this walk over the years? How many times had I taken the same route, criss crossing around graves, careful not to step on anyone? How many times had I found flowers to put in strangers' flower vases, sad that no one cared enough to come back? How many times had I cried here, laughed here, read here, and mourned here?

I looked up at the grey skies, glorifying in that sight of charcoal, layers of smudges overlapping each other. I was hungry for that shade of red in this world.

That's when I saw him.

My body froze, heart pumped, blood pounding.

"Ben?"

People talk about the world standing still all the time, and I suppose it's different for everyone. But for me, everything really did stop.

And then started back again in one painful blink.

The flash of ginger moved so fast it took a further second to realise it was coming straight for me.

I dropped my bag just in time to catch the ball of fur that clung onto my chest, claws digging into skin, confirming the dream.

I fell to my knees and started to cry.

A pain so fierce slashed into my core and left again, and I realised what it was- relief. It flooded into me, chasing after the pain, heating up the coldness within and making my limbs useless. That part of me that had been missing was suddenly lodged back in place.

The congregation started to mill into the church, staring at the strange woman hugging her cat. But I didn't care. Everything had become ok in one agonising moment of joy. I realised then, that I felt as though my soul had been shoved back into my body. It hurt. It hurt so badly. All that joy that had been starved from my body heaved back in one agonising heap of breath.

Thank you, God. Thank you, thank you, thank you. I walked with him over to my Granddad's grave and sat down, clinging to him hard as he purred in my arms, terrified to let go.

"I've been waiting here for ages," Ben meowed, licking my chin. "What took you so long?"

"What?" I looked at the flowers on the grave before me and found a little nest. Touching it, I found it still warm. "How did you get here?"

He meowed again and rubbed his face on my neck.

"How Ben? I've been so worried!"

"You don't need to know, my silly human," he purred, "but know that I've missed you."

I searched him then all over for injuries and found none. "You were gone," I said finally, tears making my skin sting.

"No I wasn't," he said simply. "I was always there."

"What? I looked everywhere!"

"And now you've found me."

I shook my head, never thinking I was going to find the answer.

"You need to accept that sometimes things happen that can't be explained," Ben said, flicking his tail. "Sometimes the explanation just doesn't exist. There's light and dark, Ellena, and you went into a place where I couldn't follow, but could only wait the other side. You had to bring yourself out of that."

"Does that mean we can start our lives now?"

"Yes."

I picked him up then, all of that black running away from me. I leant over my Granddad's headstone and kissed it.

"Love you, Granddad."

When I got home, I decided to take the U.C.W up on its offer of new employment. I also called my parents and said that yes, I would like to come to Australia, with Ben's blessing.

Emily had come back from travelling and she moved into the flat to look after Ben. He wasn't too happy at first, until he learnt she was bringing her female cat Juniper with her.

Then one day, as I was packing, I realised something as I watched Ben groom himself.

"Ben?" I said.

No answer.

"Ben?" I rolled my eyes. "*Benedict?*"

"Yesssss?"

"Since when did you get your balls back?"

He paused his grooming. "They were a gift," he said, jumping from the sofa, tail high in the air. "And if you think you're chopping them off, you've got another thing coming!"

Before I could question him, there was a knock on the door. I opened it and saw Calloway.

"Oh, hi," I said, suddenly aware that my hair was a mess and I was wearing a Game of Thrones T-shirt. "How are you?"

"Good," he said. He paused then, looking uncomfortable, scanning me quickly up and down. "You're looking well."

"Do you want to come in?"

"Sure."

I walked back into the house and put the kettle on, tidying the kitchen in a hurry before he walked in. "Tea?"

"Please." He cleared his throat and walked in behind me, ceasing my pretend cleaning. "You going somewhere?"

"Oh, Australia," I said. "But just for a month or so," I quickly added, seeing his expression of disappointment.

"Oh, good." He cleared his throat again. God, why did he look so nervous? "I err, I read the papers," he said. "I hear you have your cat back. Miracle that."

I raised my eyebrows in agreement. "I know. Crazy, huh?"

Ben walked in then, rubbing himself against Calloway's leg. The detective absently stroked him and started talking about how Ben must have walked from Stratford. It was the same story the newspapers had mused. Whether it was true, I don't know, but the fact that Ben had mysteriously grown balls over the time we were apart- that was purely divine intervention.

"My mate Emily is going to be staying here while I'm gone to look after Ben," I explained to Calloway. "But feel free to pop in anytime."

He nodded, still looking anxious. "Ok. Look, I, err, I wanted to ask you if..."

I frowned at him, watching him scratch the back of his neck until it finally dawned on me.

"I was wondering if..."

Ben meowed loudly.

"Ben, shut up," I snapped.

"I had best go," Calloway said suddenly, looking at his watch. "I can see now's not a good time anyway. Maybe I'll see you when you come back?"

"Oh... ok," I said, disappointment seeping in.

Ben meowed again.

Calloway stared at him again. "That cat looks different to when the last time I saw him," he said slowly.

I raised an eyebrow tiredly. "Yeah, he's got more bollocks than what he did before."

Calloway left before I could tell what he was going to say. I watched him through the curtains as he walked to his parked car outside, shaking his head. He glanced up briefly, catching me staring. I jumped back, shoving the curtain back in place. By the time I glanced back, he was already driving away.

Ben promised me that he wouldn't go anywhere and to be here when I returned. The flight to Perth was exhausting, but I was so happy to see my parents when I got there. I had been to Australia before but that had been Queensland. It was just wonderful spending very day in the sun with my mother, talking about the future, my job, Rowan- men.

I thought of Calloway a lot when I was away. He was a nice guy- not to mention he had saved my life. Sometimes I had nightmares about Rino. I would wake sweating, but would tell myself it was because of the Australian heat and nothing to do with the twisted perp that had tried to shoot me and set Emily alight.

I sent Emily postcards and posted them to her and Ben, asking Emily to read them out to him as well. She sent me a message via Facebook, telling me that he and Juniper were getting on very well- sometimes too well. She was having trouble keeping them apart and was planning on taking Juniper to the vets to be neutered.

Good thing too. I supposed Ben was a bit keen to try out his new balls.

I dreamt of Granddad often, but they were always nice dreams. I had a few emails from the college, telling me of their plans for the course. I managed to draft up a few plans, having everything I needed in Australia to plan the course- namely the internet, I promised to be back for enrolment, but a month passed after another and soon the time was coming closer.

One night, I got drunk and I told my dad how much I loved him.

"I want you to know how much I appreciate you," I slurred. It was ok being drunk, because we all were. Mum was in the kitchen, cutting up some cheese for crackers and getting another bottle of wine for us all. "You," I said pointing a finger to him, "are the best."

He gave me a cuddle and told me how proud he was of me. I was amazed then at how far I had come.

"Listen, we're thinking of spending another year here and then coming back," he said.

"Why?" I asked, almost choking on the newly poured wine.

"Because your mother and I want to spend more time with you and the rest of the family," he said, mum sitting next to him.

"Rowan is our first grandson. We want to be there," mum added. "Plus, we want to be there when you make those steps in your life."

My eyes widened. "I'm not having a baby, mum!" I laughed, "Not yet anyway- I haven't even got a boyfriend-"

"Yeah well," my dad said, stuffing some cheese into his mouth. "I reckoned that detective was sweet on you."

They both laughed then at my evident blush.

"I reckon you should write a book on your life, Ellena," Andy laughed. "You don't need the fantasy of Lord of the Rings- your story is enough."

"Andy, I would have done anything for Gandalf in those moments," I said jokingly.

A second's laughter passed and suddenly I realised I had said the wrong thing. My mother burst into tears, and soon I was hugging her, apologising.

"It's not that, Ellena," she sobbed. "I'm just so proud of you."

Andy clenched my arm hard and nodded, tears shining in his own eyes. "We both are."

It was hard saying goodbye, but not as hard as it would have been if I hadn't have known they were planning on coming back. I was exhausted when I arrived back at Birmingham airport, but not enough to forget I had an amazing tan. My hair had lightened and grown longer- finally to a length that my Granddad would have approved of, and I had gained some much needed weight. I looked good, but most of all, I felt it in my bones.

My sister came to pick me up, and I am ashamed to say I cried as soon as I saw her with Rowan.

"God, he's grown so much!"

Kayleigh had lost weight and it suited her. "He keeping you up?"

She nodded at me with raised eyebrows. "Something like that."

We talked about Australia and pretty much everything in between. I would be lying if I said I didn't fall asleep in the car. When I woke we were outside my flat. I was excited to see Ben when I walked up the steps to my door, and boy was I in for a surprise.

"Hi everyone!" I called opening the door.

Emily was sitting on the sofa, looking incredibly nervous. She jumped up and ran over to me to take my bags. "Hello! Did you have a good time?"

"Yeah, it was brilliant thanks- ooft!" A ball of orange fur jumped into my chest and I laughed as Ben started meowing in my ear. "Awww, I missed you too," I said. "Phew, I'm knackered."

I had a cup of tea and cuddled Emily's very fat cat Juniper. I was surprised that Ben wasn't jealous and thought it was quite nice when he cuddled up next to us.

We watched the end of Only Fools and Horses and sat together in easy silence. I asked her how things had been since she had moved in the spare room, and she said she had really enjoyed it.

"It's much better than getting a bus every day into town for work," she admitted. "I was actually thinking of getting myself a flat in the town centre."

"Yeah? Well, I'm thinking of moving out of this one," I said, not even aware I was thinking that until I said it. "You can have this one if you want to."

"What? Really? Why? Are you?"

Emily's questions threatened to boggle my already strained mind. "Um, yeah, I think... I think it's time for a fresh start for me and Ben." I paused. "I think a new flat would be good. I'm getting a new job in the summer term, which will be better pay."

"Oh brilliant," breathed Emily. "I'm thinking of settling as well. I was going to go back to Thailand with my friends but... I'm still thinking about it."

I yawned and stretched, glad for normal conversation. "I think I'm gonna go to bed."

I awoke the next day, showered and decided to clean the house. Emily had moved out and taken her cat, although still acting a bit weird.

"Finally!" expelled Ben. "How are you? Did you have a good time? I missed you! Feed me!"

He got his wish, his favourite whiskers meal, lots of cuddles and I even brushed his coat out for him. He purred as I continued to clean the house. It was June and pretty warm, so I was wearing my short shorts and an oversized pink t shirt that came over one shoulder. For the first time I felt "fixed". I even put the radio on as I cleaned and started singing. Ben joined in as well, until I was sure we were causing a huge racket.

It was long until the neighbours started banging on the door.

"Whoops!" I said, turning down the radio a touch and running to the door. "Sorry! Was I too-"

Calloway stood outside the door, hands in pockets. He gawked at me for a second and then quickly regained his composure.

"Um, hi," he said, in a smart black suit. "I finished work early and thought I would see if you were in."

"I am indeed."

"You look well."

"I'm feeling well," I grinned. "Tea?"

"Thanks."

It felt different this time letting him inside the house after everything. I felt more confident somehow. I was different, I had evolved, become stronger, wiser-harder. I had stared into death and survived. Now I was staring at Calloway, I found my lips dry. He looked good. He had a bit more colour to his face and smelt deliciously like mint and man.

I walked into the kitchen, Calloway close behind me.

"Listen, I think we might be out of tea," I said turning round, "but we have-"

The next thing I knew, Calloway's lips were on mine and my back was against the fridge. His hands pulled me hard against him, my body surrendering in surprise.

"I don't care about the tea," he said, pulling away momentarily.

"I don't either," I answered, and hauled him back.

For a while, I allowed myself to get swept away in the moment. My insides heated up and flared, filling my body with a need that I hadn't felt for a long time. I pressed my body against his and then, to my horror, I started to giggle.

I opened my eyes, and was surprised to see him smiling.

"What's so funny?" he asked.

"You took your time."

He had the grace to look embarrassed for a moment. "It's something I've wanted to do for a long while," he admitted. "I've been kicking myself over not asking you out ever since you left for Australia. I thought you weren't going to come back."

"You want to ask me out on a date?"

He kissed me again as answer.

Things after that got pretty good. I started dating Detective Calloway and I had started my first term as Head of Creative Writing. I appointed a team of local writers who started going to schools to deliver the Creative Writing Course I designed with brilliant results, not to mention I had moved back to the village my sister lived in. It was nice seeing Rowan grow up every day, with Ben at my feet. I finally had my car back from my uncle, and Ben, when he wasn't feeling too lazy, came with me to work- I had that drafted in my contract.

Sounds ridiculous? That's what happens when the cat saves the day. We had it covered over "therapy animal", which was true in a way. He kept me calm and focused- not to mention he was perfect for causing distractions when I needed to buy time.

Calloway was my saviour in the dark. He knew what I had been through, held me at night when I woke up in the middle of a nightmare, talked me through what happened. He had been there. He had seen me. He had saved my life- and I suppose when I hit the perp with the Jack Daniels bottle, I had saved his too.

And something else happened.

Ben became a dad.

Emily passed me the one ginger kitten from the set of six white kittens Juniper had given birth to. Apparently, she was too late by the time she went to the doctors and she had been dreading my return ever since she found out.

Calloway squeezed me to him after I set the pale ginger kitten on the floor. Ben sniffed him and looked at me with the same astonished expression I had seen on my brother in law's face when he watched Rowan sleep.

"Yeah, daddio," I told him. "He's yours to look after."

"It'll be you next!" joked Emily.

I just about choked when Calloway squeezed me again with a grin. I looked at Ben then, as the little kitten sniffed him and pounced beneath his feet. Ben patted it in bemusement and looked up at me in help.

"Count this as one of your cat lives, Ben," I told him.

"And a new one for you?" Calloway murmured in my ear.

I smiled. "And a new one for us."

<u>www.eearle.com</u>

More from this author...

The Adventures of Benedict and Blackwell

The Girl With Nine Lives

The Girl Who Bit Back

The Girl With Ten Claws

Stay tuned for the next instalment!

Hell Huntress

Tartarus

All queries should be sent to:

benedictandblackwell@gmail.com

Printed in Great Britain
by Amazon.co.uk, Ltd.,
Marston Gate.